The Man in the Pink Suit

The Man in the Pink Suit

Roger Silverwood

HALE CRIME

ROBERT HALE · LONDON

Typeset in 11/15 pt Janson
Printed in Great Britain by St Edmundsbury Press
Bury St Edmunds, Suffolk.
Bound by Woolnough Bookbinding Ltd

ONE

It was 1 am on Christmas Day, 2003. The sky was as black as a witch's cat. Squally winds were blowing heavy rain in all directions. Broken tree branches sailed across the hotel carpark, banging on wheel-caps and flapping against expensive bodywork, before flying over cedar-wood fencing.

Two flickering lights shone down from the eaves of the Feathers Hotel, Bromersley, picking up the twinkling reflections of a black taxi gliding through parked cars to the front door of the ivy-covered Georgian building. Rain bounced six inches from the shiny-waxed car bonnet.

The sound of a five-piece orchestra scraping through 'Auld Lang Syne' was heard momentarily over the howl of the wind as the glass doors opened and two men and a woman in evening-dress pushed their way through and down the hotel steps. The woman and the larger of the two men were supporting the older, smaller man by his arms. His feet moved uncertainly like a puppet's and his head was slumped down on to his chest. Heavy blobs of rain showered down on their backs as they packed him into the back of the taxi and closed the door.

The fat woman in a thin, tight dress stood in the pouring rain in the driveway, her hands over her head, trying to protect her twenty-five quid perm. The stark overhead lights did nothing to make her lined face look young. She shuffled her sodden, silver sandalled feet in and out of a shallow puddle.

The man pushed something at her.

Her hand came out like a striking cobra.

'Ooh, ta, sir. Thank you, and a merry Christmas.'

'Aye,' he mumbled.

The woman turned and wriggled her lumpy backside rapidly up the steps and into the hotel.

The big man sped round to the far side of the car and climbed in out of the rain.

'Where to?' the taxi driver chirped.

'The railway station. And make it quick.'

Three minutes later the car pulled into the forecourt of the small, grimy red-brick station, illuminated by a stark white light screwed high up on the crumbling wall. The driver made a semicircle, splashing through a puddle and spraying the pavement. He pulled up by a metal sign fastened to the wall. It clattered noisily as the rain beat on to it. Yellow lights illuminated the blue-and-white letters that simply read: TO TRAINS.

'There you are, guv.'

The man got out. 'How much?'

'That's a fiver to you, sir, seeing as how it's Christmas.'

The man sniffed and peeled off a note from a roll in his pocket and pointed to the figure slumped and silent in the back of the cab.

'Here's ten. Take him to 61 Sheffield Road.'

The driver smiled like a dead tortoise. 'Right boss, and a merry Christmas to you.'

The man held down his hat and danced over the puddles to the train waiting in the station.

The taxi driver switched the windscreen-wipers on to full

speed and looked back at the somnolent passenger in the back seat. He sniffed, turned his head out of the haze of brandy, and let in the clutch.

It was only a few streets to Sheffield Road; he was there in two minutes. His weary eyes peered between the windscreen wipers and the explosions of raindrops on the glass. The filaments in the streetlights made bright star-shapes on the car bonnet. He rubbed the windscreen with a rag and narrowed his eyes. The road consisted of a few terrace houses and dowdy second-position shops and offices with accommodation above. He leaned forward and peered, trying to read the property numbers. He could make out a sign that said Ogden & Company, Office Suppliers, numbers fifty-five to fifty-seven, then a florist's shop, number fifty-nine. When he arrived at sixty-one, his eyeballs shot up to his eyebrows, as he picked out the words: HAROLD PEWSKI & SON, FUNERAL DIRECTORS.

He pulled a face and licked his lips. He scratched his head and wondered if he had been given the wrong address. He shrugged. Somebody had to live there.

He pulled on the handbrake and turned round to the comatose brandy-bottle in the back.

'We're here, sir. Sixty-one,' he said tentatively.

The strong, distinctive smell billowed across to the driver's nostrils.

The passenger didn't move.

The heavy rain pounded on the car roof like the timpani in the *1812*.

The driver leaned over to the back and stretched out an arm to try to reach the man to waken him. It was too far.

'This is it, Jack. Come on. Look, you've had *your* Merry Christmas. Let me go home and have mine.'

The passenger did not reply.

'Come on!' he called loudly. The passenger remained motionless.

The driver looked out at the rain, pulled a face, groaned and banged the steering wheel hard with both hands. He muttered something and it wasn't Shakespeare. Then he reached down to the shelf under the dashboard, found a baseball cap, pulled it tight on to his head and turned up his suit coat collar. He got out of the cab hanging on to the door, closed it with both hands and turned to face the driving rain. Holding on to his cap, he swiftly leapt over a puddle and round to the back of the taxi. He yanked open the rear passenger door.

'Here we are, sir. Now come on,' he pleaded. 'There's nothin' to pay.'

The passenger was propped against the door, and, as it opened, his head and shoulders flopped heavily sideways out of the car. His body followed and then, with increasing momentum, the little man rolled into the gutter with a splash.

He was dead.

On the 6th September 2004, Charles Tabor opened the newspaper on his desk and glanced at the front page. The *Daily Chronicle* was always good for a topical story, especially if it was supported by an uncommon photograph. It specialized in features that embarrassed celebrities and Members of Parliament, and struck out at the establishment.

Tabor's eyebrows lifted when he saw the photograph of a man on his knees on the pavement by the open door of a limousine. The man's eyes were screwed up, his mouth open, and his hand was reaching out towards the camera. There was the side view of a woman reaching down to him. She had long fair hair and a short dress, revealing heavy legs. From the reflections and the background, the photograph had been taken in the dark with a flash.

Tabor sat down at his desk to savour the article printed beneath it. He read:

EX 'BOOZE' BOSS TRIPS!

Cabinet Minister in the gutter

The Right Honourable Eric Weltham, MP, PC, 45, Minister for R & D slipped on the pavement and fell in the gutter while getting into a car in the rain outside Fenella's Nightclub in the West End of London last night. The MP for Bromersley South had earlier been seen dancing and dining with his latest girlfriend, Louella Panter, the glamorous host of TV's newest big money panel game, *What's in it for me?*

A photographer, who was passing, covering an unrelated story, took this exclusive pic.

He asked the MP if he was ill and needed a doctor. The Cabinet Minister said, 'B***** off.'

The photographer then asked if he had been drinking.

The Minister replied, 'If you publish that b***** photograph I'll sue you for every penny you've got!'

Miss Panter, who tore her tights while assisting Mr Weltham to his feet, bundled him into the car with the help of her young, blond security man, who then drove the embarrassed couple away quickly in the direction of Park Lane.

Visitors to Fenella's said that the couple had been there more than two hours, and that they had seen the couple drinking and dancing. It was thought that they had consumed several bottles of wine.

Frank P Jones, art critic and bon viveur, known as 'the man in pink', who was dining alone, commented: 'I have no idea who the fat girl is. I have never heard of her or her programme.'

The manager of Fenella's refused to make any comment.

Eric Weltham was appointed to the newly created Cabinet

post last February. Earlier this year, it was reported that his failed drinks and casinos group, Boozers And Winners, went into liquidation with debts of over a million pounds.

His second wife of four years is understood to be seeking a divorce. His twenty-year-old son from his first marriage was charged with drunken driving and given community service in December last.

Eric Weltham has held the seat in Bromersley South for ten years with successively reduced majorities at each of the three elections. At the last election fourteen months ago, his majority was down to 1,805.

The corners of Charles Tabor's mouth turned up. He nodded several times, lowered the newspaper, folded it and tossed it to the corner of the big desk.

Pretty Ingrid Dooley came through the open office door carrying a letter file. She stood at the desk and looked down at the big man.

'There's Mr Coldwell to see you, from accounts, Mr Tabor. And I've finished your letters.'

'Right. I'll sign them now. He can wait,' he said, running a hand over his forehead and back over his receding hairline.

Ingrid put the file on the desk in front of him and opened it at the first letter.

Charles Tabor clicked his pen and began reading. He stopped briefly and, without looking up, said:

'I want you to get me the telephone number of our illustrious MP and cabinet minister, Eric Weltham.'

He sniffed and with a rapid flourish of the wrist, applied his signature to a letter.

'Do you want me to get him on the line?'

He lifted up his eagle-shaped nose. 'No. Just get me his London number.'

'Right, sir.'

He scratched away at the letters, then leaned back from the desk and replaced the top on his pen.

Ingrid closed the folder and picked it up. He pulled a face and sniffed again. 'Right,' he said, 'send Coldwell in.'

She made for the door and came back a moment later, leading a small man.

'Mr Coldwell, sir.'

'Come in, Coldwell. Sit down.'

'Good morning, Mr Tabor,' the man said with the look of a startled rabbit.

'Morning. Now, Coldwell, how old are you?'

'Fifty-eight, sir.'

'Mmm. Yes,' Tabor replied heavily. 'I'm prepared to be very generous to you because of your age.'

The little man blinked and licked his lips. He gripped the arms of the chair tightly.

'I don't *want* to leave, Mr Tabor,' he said in a small voice.

Tabor glared across the desk at him. 'You're making too many mistakes. You have to.'

'I only made the one, sir. And I found it, and put it right before the accounts were sent out.'

'One mistake is one too many. Besides that, you are slow. Anyway, I am not arguing about it. As I said, I'm prepared to make you a substantial one-off payment. Call it a golden handshake, if you like. Five thousand pounds. In cash. How's that?'

Coldwell's eyes lit up. A big smile expanded his small, round twitching orifice.

'Most generous, Mr Tabor. Most generous. Well, thank you, sir.'

The big man looked at the door. 'Ingrid!'

Miss Dooley put her nose round the doorjamb.

'A discharge form,' he said, raising a hand.

She nodded and left.

Tabor reached forward on the desk and picked up two keys with shafts ten inches or so long. He crossed the room to a black lacquered Chinese cabinet set on a marble stand in the corner of the office. He opened the double doors to reveal the front of a steel safe. Thick blue and red plastic-covered wires were fitted across the door of the safe, and threaded round the side to the back, out of sight. He inserted the long keys, one above the other and pushed them deep into the thick casing of the safe. He turned them, and then pulled open the door with a brass handle. He reached in and picked up five Cellophane packets. Each packet was printed: Northern Bank. £1,000. He tossed them on to the desk in front of the starry-eyed man.

'Oooh. Thank you, sir.'

Tabor locked the safe door and withdrew the keys.

'You have to sign a receipt absolving the company from any further salary or pension liability. This is payment in full. It includes absolutely all payments due to you. Severance pay, holiday pay, pension rights, everything. And you don't have to work a notice period. You finish work today. Is that understood?'

'Oh yes, Mr Tabor. Most generous.'

Ingrid came in with the discharge form.

'Right. Read it. It's all written down there. And sign it at the bottom.'

The little man began writing.

'You want to put that money somewhere safe.'

'Oh yes, Mr Tabor. I'm not taking any chances. I'll go straight up to the Mercantile bank with it.'

'Take a taxi.'

'Oh? Er, yes.'

'I shall order one for you.' Tabor picked up the phone and

dialled a number. 'This is Charles Tabor here. Is that the taxi company? I want you to collect a valued ex-employee and deliver him safely to the Mercantile bank.... Yes. The bank. Do you understand? He's leaving my office now.'

He replaced the phone and looked at the little man who was stuffing the money in his pockets.

'A taxi will pick you up outside the front doors in five minutes,' Charles Tabor said, then he crossed to another door leading directly into the hallway. He opened it and beckoned the little man to go through it.

'Oh. Thank you, Mr Tabor, sir,' he said, nodding and smiling. 'Thank you very much. Good day to you, sir. Good day.'

'Goodbye,' the big man said brusquely and closed the door. He smirked with satisfaction as he returned to the desk. He knew the £5,000 would be back in his safe before the end of the day.

Ingrid Dooley came into the office waving a slip of paper.

'The private London number of that MP, Eric Weltham, is ex-directory, sir. But I have the number for the Ministry of Research and Development.'

She put the paper on the desk in front of him.

'Right,' Charles Tabor said. He reached over to the telephone on his desk. His podgy, soft, manicured fingers stabbed at the phone-buttons.

T W O

'More brandy?'

Eric Weltham, MP for Bromersley South, held forth the huge glass across the dining-table.

'Why not, Charles? Why not?'

Tabor took the six-inch cigar out of his mouth, and poured an adequate triple measure into his guest's glass and a single into his own.

The MP dragged the napkin up from his lap and wiped his mouth.

'That was a delightful meal, Charles. I thought I had been to all the best eating-houses in the city, but this is a new one to me. I suppose you have to be a member of the club?'

'Oh yes.'

'And to get a private room like this, book well in advance?'

Tabor looked down his nose over his spectacles.

'Or over-tip the restaurant manager,' he said pointedly.

Eric Weltham thought for a moment and then smiled.

'Yes. Of course.' He relaxed back in the chair, sipping the brandy and occasionally shaking his head with eyes half-closed, hoping the lobster would soon find a position in his stomach that it liked.

Charles Tabor pulled at the cigar, drummed his hand on the

THE MAN IN THE PINK SUIT

crisp tablecloth for a few seconds before he broke the silence. He forced a smile and said:

'You're good company, Eric,' he lied. 'There's no wonder you're so popular.'

Weltham looked across the table at him. He shook his head.

'Popular? Huh! I'm not popular.'

'Women *like* you. They flock round you,' Tabor nodded reassuringly, with a smile that could have been mistaken for a sneer.

'Don't talk to me about women,' he replied, shaking his head.

'Oh? I couldn't help but read about your exploits with the delectable Louella Panter.'

Weltham smiled. 'Ah yes. Now *she*'s all right,' he said briefly. He took a sip of the brandy and looked vaguely at the burgundy flocked wallpaper at the far side of the room. He smiled again and shook his head thoughtfully. 'Women,' he said for no reason at all.

Tabor pursed his lips, his ears attuned.

'You should ask my wife about me,' said Weltham. 'Oh yes.' He paused deliberately, and then continued: 'Oh no. Huh. On second thoughts, you shouldn't ask my wife about me. You are too much of a gentleman to hear such language!' He laughed at what he considered was a great joke.

Tabor permitted his lips to turn up at the corners slightly. After a moment, he sniffed and then said quietly:

'Women can be *so* unreasonable.'

'I'll say,' Weltham replied, coming out of the glass. 'It's funny you should say that, Charles. Yes. Funny you should say that,' he replied, swilling the brandy around. 'Have you any idea what my wife wants in the way of a settlement?'

'No.'

'She wants the house, and a five-figure sum, annually, until she's seventy-five! What do you think to that?'

Tabor screwed up his eyebrows and shook his head slightly.

'And what's more,' Weltham continued. 'She wants it index-linked to the cost of living!'

Tabor pursed his lips in sympathy.

'She's been watching too much bloody politics on television!! I didn't know she knew what index-linked meant. What's happened to equal rights? It would be cheaper to stay married to her!'

Tabor nodded.

'And I might just have to do that,' Weltham muttered. 'Dammit!' He stuck his nose in the glass again. 'I'm still paying my first wife, Greta,' he continued after a slurp. 'Now there *was* a woman. A real woman. She's still got her looks, as well. She's forty-two, you know. She's the mother of my son, Charles. My only son. Mmm. Yes. And he's costing me a fortune at that poncy university. I tell you, it's all pay, pay, pay!'

'But you get a good screw as a cabinet minister, Eric?'

'I do. I do. But it is soon spent. You have to keep up with everything, you know. And I have commitments. I have to keep three homes going. And it's not like living in Bromersley, you know. My flat in Westminster costs me a bomb.'

'But there are perks.'

'Perks? The only perks I get is the chauffeur and car.' He dived into the glass again and drained it. Then he added quickly: 'So I get a free trip to Swansea or Todmorden or somewhere now and again. So what? If it was Monte Carlo or Rio de Janeiro, then that would be something, wouldn't it? Hey! Is there any more brandy?'

'Yes, of course. Plenty.'

Tabor picked up the bottle and discovered it was empty. His eyebrows went up. 'Oh. Soon fix that.'

He picked up the small gilt bell on the table and shook it. It made a little, high-pitched tinkle.

'I'm sure things will go well for you from now on. After all, ten years ago – isn't it? – you were working in a glass-factory: now you're a Cabinet Minister! If that isn't a success story, I don't know what is.'

A bald-headed waiter came in with a crisp towel over his sleeve. Charles Tabor was waiting for him. He held the empty brandy-bottle out to him.

'Fill that up, will you, son?' he said. 'And make it quick.'

The waiter nodded and went out.

Weltham swirled the empty brandy-glass round.

'That's true. I'll be all right if I can retain my seat and my office at the next election. If the government becomes unpopular, as they do, after three terms in office, it'll not be easy hanging on to a marginal like Bromersley South, I can tell you.'

'There's some years to run of this government, Eric. As a high-profile cabinet minister and Privy Councillor, you'll become even better known than you are now. That exposure will provide you with all kinds of opportunities to mix in commercial circles and increase your earnings capacity for the time when you retire from politics.'

'I expect you are right, Charles. I expect you're right,' Weltham said, clearly unconvinced. He shook his head several times and then said: 'But you see, old chap, I need funds now!' He swung the glass in the air. 'Where's that brandy?' he called.

'It's coming.'

This was the opportunity Tabor had been waiting for. He rubbed the lobe of an ear between finger and thumb.

'Really?' he said. 'Mmm. As a matter of fact, I may be able to help you there, Eric.'

Weltham's eyes clicked open.

'Help me? That would be nice, for someone to help *me* for a change.'

'Oh yes. Why not? We are friends aren't we?'

'What have you in mind?' Weltham asked brightly.

Tabor pushed a plate and knife away from him.

'As you know, my business in Bromersley is doing very well. I don't intend to let the grass grow under my feet. I'm in an expansionist mood, Eric. Computers are here to stay. They are the commercial miracle of today. I am going upwards and onwards.'

Weltham nodded. 'Why not? Why not? Strike while the iron's hot! Make hay while the sun shines, what?!'

Charles Tabor beamed. His quarry could not have spoken a truer word. He licked his lips, leaned forward as he began to set the trap.

'I have noted with obvious interest the advertisements for tenders to supply your Ministry, Research and Development, with several hundred computers, printers and scanners.'

Weltham screwed his eyebrows upwards and grunted. 'Oh yes. Yes.'

'And I am in the business,' Tabor smiled.

The MP pursed his lips. 'Oh. But I can't do anything about that, Charles,' he said, shaking his head.

'I know. I know. Hear me out.'

'Where's the brandy?'

On cue, the waiter came in with the bottle on a silver tray. He went over to the service table, wrapped the bottle in a towel and began to withdraw the cork

'Requisitions of that sort are matters entirely for the Civil Service,' Weltham said as he pulled the cigar out of his mouth and looked round at the waiter. 'Yes. They're for *my* Ministry, but I just rubber-stamp their proposals.'

'Of course. Of course. I thought that would be the case. But, you do *see* the tenders, don't you?'

'Yes.'

The waiter came forward with the bottle held at the ready. 'Brandy, sir?'

Weltham held up his glass. The waiter poured a generous measure.

'That's it, son,' Weltham said, pulling the glass away from the bottle and up to his lips.

The waiter turned to Charles Tabor. 'For you, sir?'

'Put the bottle down and leave us,' Tabor said brusquely. He waved the man away.

'Very good, sir. Will there be anything else?'

'No.'

The waiter bowed and made for the door.

'Well, Eric, if I knew the contents of the other tenders, I would easily be able to meet and beat their prices and terms. The only serious competition I have is from American companies. Well, I don't have to deliver from the other side of the world. My production costs in Bromersley are far lower than theirs. And my prices are much lower than theirs. And my business is all British capital, you know. It isn't a British office selling parts of US patterns with US money. Oh no. And do you know, Eric, the savings I would make on landing this order, this year alone, would amount to around a hundred thousand pounds. If I secure the order, it wouldn't half please your constituents, wouldn't it? To know that their jobs were even more secure, eh?

'Of course, some of your constituents work for me. Wouldn't they be pleased if they knew you were the blue-eyed boy who helped to secure their jobs and pushed work locally? It would go down well at the next election, too, wouldn't it? It would drive your popularity up. It would certainly mean more votes! And I could pass that saving on to the one who had the wisdom, the foresight *and* the patriotism to help me keep that order here in Britain, in Bromersley, in *your* constituency. And I could pass that saving on to you!'

Eric Weltham's jaw dropped.

'What? Did you say, a hundred thousand pounds?'

'That's this year. Could be more next year. What with repeats, add-ons, service, etcetera. And all I need is sight of the other tenders. That's all. In fact, I don't need to see the originals. Photocopies would do. The originals need never leave your office.'

Weltham breathed in deeply and expired noisily.

'It sounds very risky.'

'Not at all. There'd be absolutely no risk if I paid you in cash, would there.'

'Cash?'

'Yes. Literally cash. Tens. Twenties. There'd be no trace back to its source. Nothing in writing. No witnesses. No third party. No leaks. What could go wrong?'

Weltham rubbed his chin. His thumb and fingers excitedly danced on the stem of his glass.

Charles Tabor's dark-blue eyes stared across at him observing every reaction. He leaned forward. 'You could pay your wife off,' he added. 'Pay your son's expenses at university. And, in the highly unlikely event of your not being returned at the next election, it would help cushion any loss of office, wouldn't it.' He slapped down an open hand on the tabletop. 'And think of the honeymoon you and Miss Panter could have with that sort of money. And nobody has to know anything about it.'

Charles Tabor reached out for the brandy-bottle, poured himself two fingers, drank it in one gulp and replaced the glass firmly on the table with a flourish.

'Just think about it, Eric,' he said blowing a cloud of smoke across the room.

Weltham pursed his lips and said nothing. His pulse raced. His thoughts whizzed round his head faster than a bee in a bottle.

The telephone rang.

'CID. Cadet Ahaz speaking,' the young man said in a very precise voice. 'No sir. Detective Inspector Angel is with the Chief Constable.'

Ahmed Ahaz felt a hand on his shoulder.

'Not any more, lad. I'm here. What is it?' the DI said brusquely.

The Indian looked up from his chair at the big man.

'Oh.' He turned back to the phone. 'Please hold on, sir.'

'Who is it?' growled Angel.

'It's the super. He wants to see you. It's very urgent.'

Angel's bushy eyebrows moved upwards.

'Tell him I'm on my way.' He left the office and shot down the olive-green police-station corridor to the last door on the right. A printed plastic sign was screwed on to the door. It read, SUPERINTENDENT J. HARKER. Angel knocked, opened the door and pushed his head into the little office.

Another big man with a head shaped like a turnip, and with short white hair was seated at a desk. He waved Angel in as he replaced the phone.

'You wanted me, John?'

'A woman has just rung in. Triple-nine call. A secretary. Ingrid Dooley. A man has been shot in an office at Tabor Industries. On that new industrial estate.'

'I know it.' Angel turned to go.

'She's sent for an ambulance. I'll send forensics, SOCOs and some uniformed.'

'Right, sir.' He closed the door and hurried up the corridor to the CID room. The door was wide open. He glanced inside. It was unusually quiet. Three plain-clothes men were in a corner in deep conversation. The young Cadet Ahmed Ahaz, was seated at the computer on a long bench-table near the door, concentrating on the screen and tapping the keys.

'Where's DS Gawber, lad?' Angel puffed.

Ahmed turned round. 'He's gone to the hospital, sir.'

'What?' roared Angel. 'What for?'

'Fell down, sir.'

'Fell down?' Angel roared again.

The three detectives at the far end of the room looked across. Angel noticed but ignored them.

'He was coming in through the back entrance and slipped on that sloping path on the ice,' Ahmed explained. 'It was a nasty fall.'

'Did you see it happen?'

'No, sir.'

'Well how do you know it was a nasty fall?'

Ahmed gawped at him.

'Never mind. See if you can raise him on his mobile. Tell him to meet me at Tabor Industries, smartish. A man's been shot.'

Cadet Ahmed Ahaz's jaw dropped. '*Shot*, sir?'

Angel turned to leave. He turned back. 'Have you got that, lad?'

'Oh. Yes sir.'

'*Well do it then!*' bellowed Angel.

'Yes sir.' Ahmed's eyes flashed as he reached out for the phone.

Angel arrived at his own office, put on his raincoat, shoved his leather-backed notepad in his pocket and went through the rear exit, down the slope and into the yard.

He knew that the Tabor Industries factory was sited on the Northrop industrial estate north of Bromersley. He pointed his car in that direction and was on the estate service-road in four minutes. He soon found the place. It was a large, new, brick-built factory with the words: TABOR INDUSTRIES, in bold letters within a huge outline of a computer as its logo, fixed to the front wall. The high roof was covered with melting snow which was slithering down the tiles. An ambulance was standing on a yellow-hatched area, by the entrance. Angel speeded up to park his car alongside it. Water from thawing snow dripped on his neck as he reached the big glass automatic doors which opened in front of him. He glanced down the entrance hall. The area was deserted. It was bright, clean and businesslike, warmly illuminated by six concealed wall lights. At the far end was a long counter with the word *Reception* above it.

Behind the desk, lights from a small PBX flashed impatiently. On one side of the counter was a lift door and on the other an open staircase with a pedestal sign with the words 'To Offices'. A big palm-tree in a small pot stood at the bottom of the stairway. Suspended from the ceiling and focused on him was a CCTV camera. He made for the stairs and was soon at the top. There were four doors on the landing, all wide open. He could hear hushed voices as he reached the nearest door. He rushed into the office and quickly took in the scene.

Two ambulance men were kneeling, attending a man on a green flowered carpet by a large desk. One man was unwrapping a stethoscope, the other pressing a padded dressing over the man's chest. Bright red streaks of blood marked his shirt, his coat and the carpet. The man's eyes were closed. He was very still. He had lost a lot of blood.

Angel pursed his lips and shook his head. He looked around the room. Four young women were huddled in one corner of the office, whispering and occasionally glancing towards the man on the floor. A man in a white coat and a pretty woman stood anxiously near the desk, also looking down at the bleeding man. The young woman was dabbing her face with a handkerchief from time to time. This was a large, expensively furnished office with one big desk, a swivel-chair and four other chairs, a filing-cabinet and a black Chinese cabinet against a wall. Behind the desk, a big window overlooked a double-glazing factory on the opposite side of the road next to a wholesale stationers at the side of a petrol service-station. The office had three doors, one in each of the other interior walls. A red light flashed irregularly from a CCTV camera high in the corner of the room directed towards the desk.

As Angel made for the medics, the young woman left the man in the white coat and came over to him.

'Are you the police?'

'Yes.'

She put her hand up to mouth. It was shaking slightly.

'I phoned you. I dialled 999.'

Angel said, 'Just a minute, love.'

He went over to the side of the desk where the injured man lay. He leaned over the shoulder of one of the ambulance men, who had a stethoscope on the man's chest. 'I'm DI Angel, Bromersley CID,' he said quietly. 'How is he?'

'Give us a minute, guv.'

'Right.'

Angel turned back to the young lady and pointed at the bloodied man on the floor.

'Who's that?'

'Mr Tabor. The boss. *My* boss.'

'And who are you?'

'I'm Ingrid Dooley, his secretary.'

'Did you see what happened?'

'No. I was out of the office at the time.'

The young man in the white coat and spectacles came over. 'Is he going to be all right? I'm his son, Mark Tabor.'

'I don't know,' Angel said quietly. 'Did you see what happened?'

'No.'

Angel noticed the ambulance men packing up their instruments. He leaned over to them.

'How bad is it?' he whispered.

'Gunshot wound. He's in a bad way. We'll have to move him. We can't do any more for him here.'

'Mmm. Is he conscious?'

'He keeps slipping in and out.'

'Can I talk to him?'

'You can try. We've got to get him to theatre.'

They dashed off carrying bags.

Angel's eyes followed them out of the door. He dropped down on his knees and eased his head right up close to the man. Despite the loss of blood, the man's face was red. He had a big nose and there was a crease on the bridge where his spectacles had rested. His mouth was partly open but Angel couldn't detect any breathing.

He looked up at Ingrid Dooley and Mark Tabor.

'What's his name in full?'

'Charles Tabor,' replied Ingrid.

Angel leaned close to the man's ear.

'Can you hear me, Mr Tabor?'

There was the slightest grunt.

'Who did this to you, sir?'

Another grunt.

'Mr Tabor. We can catch him, if we know who it is. What is his name? Whisper it.'

Angel quickly put his ear an inch away from Tabor's lips.

He waited. There was something. Angel's eyelids lifted momentarily then lowered.

The ambulance men bustled in purposefully with a stretcher.

Mark Tabor pushed forward again.

'What did he say? Did he say anything?' he asked eagerly.

Angel pursed his lips.

'Nothing. Nothing at all.' He raised himself up from the carpet and pulled away, rubbing his chin. He wandered thoughtfully over to the four women in the corner. They turned towards him. 'Did any of you see what happened?'

They crowded round him. Ingrid Dooley and Mark Tabor joined the group.

A young red-headed woman spoke up confidently.

'I saw it. It was the Man in the Pink Suit.'

'Yes. Yes,' said the others.

Out the corner of his eye, Angel saw the ambulance men manoeuvre the stretcher with Charles Tabor aboard through the office door and out of the room.

Another woman said, 'Yes. I saw it. It was him. Him that's on the telly. Does programmes about 'Art' an' that. Yes. They call him the Man in the Pink Suit.'

Another woman added: 'I saw it too. His proper name's Jones. Frank P. Jones. Lives local. It's dreadful. In broad daylight. Disgrace.'

The other women muttered agreement.

'He didn't try to hide who he was, or anything.'

'It's not safe to go out at nights in Bromersley.'

'It's not safe to come out to work in daylight!'

'What's it all coming to?'

Angel looked at the red haired woman. 'Well, what did you *actually* see?'

Her eyes opened wide, she held out her arms in front of

her. She swallowed and said: 'I saw everything. He came in
and shot Mr Tabor.'

'I saw it too.'

'And I did.'

'It was awful.'

They all started talking at once and then Angel became
aware that people were approaching him from behind. It was
Dr Mac and two of his scenes-of-crime team.

'Your case, Mike?' asked the pathologist.

'Yeah,' said Angel.

'What's happened?'

'A man called Charles Tabor was shot and he's just been
taken to the hospital.' He pointed to the door. 'You could have
passed him.'

Mac looked down at the carpet by the desk.

'Mmm. Blood.' He sniffed. 'Was he shot here?'

Angel pointed to the floor. 'There.'

Mac's mouth tightened. He glanced round the room, stuck
out a thumb at all the people there and said:

'This is a crime scene, Mike.'

'I know. I know,' Angel said impatiently. 'I'll clear it. But
I'm here on my own. Have you seen Gawber anywhere?'

'No.'

Angel saw an open door at the other end of the office. He
turned to Ingrid Dooley.

'Where's that lead to?'

'That's my office.'

'Did the man with the gun come through there?'

'No. They said he came through the general office. That's
through that door.' She nodded towards the opposite door.

'Right. I'll use your office then, if you don't mind.'

Ingrid Dooley nodded. 'I'll go out. I feel a walk will do me
good.'

Two uniformed policemen arrived at the door. Angel sighed and waved a hand. One of them came across.

'Are you in charge, sir?'

'Yes, lad. And this is the crime scene. Get everybody out of here and out of that office next door.' He turned to the other officer. 'Come with me. Have you seen DS Gawber in your travels?'

'No sir.'

Angel shook his head and growled. He led the way into Ingrid Dooley's small office. He dropped his hat on top of the filing cabinet, turned and leaned back against the desk.

'I'll see those five women and the man one at a time, Constable. Will you wheel that red hair in first?'

'Right, sir.'

The red-headed young woman stood hesitating in the doorway.

'Ah yes. Come in, love. What's your name?'

'Elizabeth Cracken.'

'Right, Elizabeth. What did you see?'

'I work in the general office through there. I was doing my work. I'm an accounts clerk. I was sat at my desk, working at a computer when the door opened and the man came in.'

'Did he knock?'

'No.'

'How was he dressed?'

'Like I said. He was dressed like he is on television. In a pink suit.'

'What else?'

'Erm … A straw-hat. Sunglasses.'

'What else? Pink shoes?'

'I don't know. I didn't notice his shoes.'

'Pink tie?'

'Yes. Dickie bow.'

'Pink shirt?'

'Yes.'

'Was he carrying anything?'

'No.'

'Are you sure about all this, Elizabeth?'

'Positive.'

'What happened?'

'He opened the door into Mr Tabor's office and went in. My desk is opposite the door so I could see what happened.'

'Go on.'

'I heard Mr Tabor shout something and I saw him stand up. The man in pink went right up to the front of the desk and pulled a gun out of his pocket. He pointed it at him, fired it once, then, still carrying it in his hand, he came back out of Mr Tabor's office through our office and out into the corridor.'

'What was the gun like?'

'I don't know anything about guns. Only what I've seen on films. Small, I suppose, and black.'

'Did you see Mr Tabor fall?'

'Yes. It was awful. It was frightening. When I heard the gunshot, I ducked down behind the desk.'

'So you didn't actually see the man come back through your office and out into the corridor.'

'Yes I did. I was on the floor peeping over the top of the desk. I saw it all.'

'Are you absolutely positive it was this man in pink, the one on television?'

'Yes.'

'You'll be asked to make a statement. And sign it.'

'Yes. I expect so.'

Angel smiled and nodded. A good witness, he thought. No shilly-shallying. She knows what she saw and isn't afraid to say so.

'Right. Thank you.'

'Can I go?'

'Leave your address before you go home, will you?'

Elizabeth Cracken left the room.

'Constable!' Angel called.

The policeman showed his nose through the door. 'Yes sir?'

'Show the next witness in, will you?'

A young blonde lady came in.

'What's your name?'

'Rachel Honeycutt.'

'What did you see, Rachel?'

'I'm the receptionist. I work at the front desk, downstairs. About an hour ago, that TV star, the man in the pink suit, came through the glass doors, passed me and he flew up the stairs. When I realized he was bypassing me, I called after him. He ignored me. Mr Tabor was a stickler for not allowing visitors into the building unannounced. I was in the process of moving some papers so that I could leave the desk and come upstairs to find him, when I heard a loud bang. I thought it must be a gun. Immediately after that, the man in pink came running down the stairs waving a gun in his hand, like in a cowboy film. He went straight out of the door.'

'Can you describe the gun?'

'Wasn't very big.'

'Hmm. How was he dressed?'

'Like he is on the television. Pink suit. Straw hat. Pink carnation in his buttonhole. Sunglasses. You know.'

'What else?'

Rachel Honeycutt screwed up her eyebrows. 'Pardon?'

Angel said: 'What colour was his shirt and tie?'

'Pink, I suppose.'

'And his shoes?'

'I'm not sure about that.'

'Were they pink?'

She shook her head. 'I think I would have noticed if they were pink. I don't think they were pink. But there was something a bit different about them. They were brown, I think. Yes. Brown.'

'Brown leather?'

She thought a moment. 'Do you know, Inspector? I think they were suede.'

Angel smiled. 'You seem pretty sure about everything else.'

'I am. Whatever he was wearing, he looked just like he does on the telly.'

'What did you do then? Did you follow him outside?'

'No. I went straight upstairs to see what had happened. I thought I might be in for trouble.'

'You didn't see what happened to him when he went outside. If he got in a car or whatever?'

'No. I never thought. I was anxious to find out what had happened upstairs.'

Angel nodded. 'Right, Miss Honeycutt, thank you.' He turned to the constable. 'I'll see Mr Mark Tabor next.'

The young man with the glasses came in. His head was shaking slightly.

'Do you know how he is, Inspector?'

'No, lad. I don't. Forgive me pressing you at this time. Did you see what happened?'

'No.'

'Hmmm. Did your father have any enemies?

'Obviously, this man,' Mark Tabor muttered angrily. 'This man in the pink suit. He's a queer, isn't he? Must be mental. This Frank P. Jones.'

'What do you know about it?'

'I believe there was an outstanding debt. Jones wouldn't pay for something he'd ordered. It goes back a long way. I'm not very sure about it. Dad deals with the accounts and all things like that. I'm responsible for the works: production and dispatch.'

'Right. If you remember any more about this, will you let me know?'

'Of course.'

'Was there anybody else who might have a grudge against him?'

'You always make enemies in business, Inspector. I don't know of anybody in particular who would feel like this about Dad.'

'Where were you at the time of the shooting?'

'I was in my office in the factory, sorting through some orders.'

'Did you hear the shot?'

'No. My office is on the ground floor at the other end of the building. When I heard, of course I came running up to see what had happened. It must have taken a few minutes for the news to reach me. Actually, somebody in the general office came through on the phone.'

'Where was Ingrid Dooley?'

'I don't know.'

'Right. We'll leave it at that for now, Mr Tabor. Thank you.'

Angel went to the other door and opened it.

Dr Mac and two other men were peeling off rubber gloves and unzipping their protective white-plastic overalls.

'Have you finished, Mac?' Angel called.

'Ay,' the Scotsman replied. 'I've finished here, just about. He lost a lot of blood. I'd like to see the wound. There's nae fingerprints. The man didn't touch anything. There's nothing here. We might get something from his shoes. I don't know. I'll let you know tomorrow.'

'Thanks, Mac.'

Angel ran his hand across his chin. This was looking like a cut-and-dried case. He closed his notepad and made his way hurriedly down the stairs. At the bottom, he stopped, looked round the reception hall and, finding it still deserted, took out his mobile phone and tapped in a number.

It was soon answered. 'DS Gawber.'

'I've been ringing you all morning. Where the hell are you?'

'I am at home sir.'

'You're harder to get than the enquiry desk at British Rail. Are you my sergeant or what?'

'Your phone must have been switched off, sir. I have tried several times to reach you. I thought Ahmed would have explained. I asked him to let you know. I fell down on the ice on that slope leading to the station back door, landed awkwardly and I've broken my ankle. I've been in casualty all morning. I've just been brought back by ambulance. '

Angel blew through pursed lips. 'Marvellous. A fat lot of good you're going to be to me. Can you walk?'

'No.'

'Can you drive?'

'No.'

'How long are you going to be like this?'

'Don't know, sir.'

'Hmm. You've got more excuses than a plumber. I can see what'll happen. I shall finish up with Crisp. I can feel it in my water. He's the only sergeant on the strength who hasn't got a regular attachment.'

'Sorry about that, sir.'

'Not half as sorry as I am, lad. Hmm. Here, while you are on, do you happen to know where that chap from the telly – the Man in the Pink Suit – lives?'

34

'The art expert? He has a house on Huddersfield Road. I don't know the number, but it's opposite the park entrance. It has a big black stone lion at each side of the front door.'

'Right lad. Get that ankle right.' He switched off the phone, dropped it in his pocket and made for the glass doors.

They opened automatically but it wasn't his movement that had triggered them. A tall, smartly dressed young man was standing outside.

Their eyes met. It was Detective Sergeant Crisp.

'There you are, sir. I've been looking for you.'

Angel pulled a face. 'Oh? What do you want, lad?'

'D S Gawber's broken his ankle, sir. Superintendent Harker has put me on your team for the time being.'

'Oh great! That's marvellous!' Angel said, his eyes shining and his fists clenched. 'Tarzan's got Cheetah, and I've got you!'

THREE

Angel despatched DS Crisp to Bromersley General Hospital to keep an eye on the victim. He didn't want to make it easy for the man in the pink suit to have an opportunity to fire off another pot-shot at Tabor.

Meanwhile, he drove off to investigate where the arty-crafty man lived. He pulled his car up in front of a big Victorian stone-faced house on the main road between Bromersley and Huddersfield and stepped out into the wet. Most of the snow had turned to water but there was a track of slush at both sides of the road. He strode over the slush, crossed the pavement, reached over the low gate and lifted the latch to admit him on to a small frontage which he conjectured had originally been a pathway through a small garden to the front door. It appeared the area had been neatly covered over with flagstones recently, to minimize maintenance for the resident who didn't enjoy gardening.

He made his way up the path to two black-painted stone lions guarding the door. He went up two steps and pressed the doorbell. He didn't know what to expect. He'd seen the Man in the Pink Suit on television occasionally and had been slightly curious because he was a local man, but he was not at all interested in his programmes or in academic art. On the evidence of four witnesses, it was inevitable that he would have to arrest him, and he hoped there would be no show of firearms. The longer he waited the more apprehensive he became and he wondered if he should have come armed. He noticed a peephole in the door and wondered if he was being stared at. Eventually, there was the sound of several bolts being drawn back, the rattle of the door furniture and then the door was opened three inches on a chain.

A thin nose, an eye and a mouth appeared through the gap. An academic high-pitched man's voice said: 'Yes?'

Angel identified the voice and demeanour of the man.

'I am Inspector Angel of Bromersley Police. Are you Frank P. Jones?'

'Yes,' the man said with a sniff.

'I need to speak to you, sir.'

The man pursed his lips. 'Who did you say you were?'

'I'm from the police.'

'Oh?' he said, his voice a little higher. The man sniffed again. 'Very well.'

The door closed briefly and then opened wide to reveal a man about forty, of lean build, with fair hair. He was wearing a pair of black tapered slacks, red smoking-jacket, a loud-checked shirt without a tie and leather slippers.

'Now, what is it?' he said, grimacing and shaking his head.

'Can we go inside, sir?' Angel asked, knowing that he was going into the house whatever the man said.

Jones stared at him closely and put up a hand, holding his fingers splayed like a cockatoo's feathers. He held the pose momentarily.

'Very well,' he said condescendingly and pulled open the door. 'Follow me.'

Angel stepped into the dark hallway.

Dark paintings in rich gilt frames looked down on him

from every wall. Heavy furniture reduced passageway down the hall to single file. Everything was spotlessly clean. There were no ornaments, vases or flowers.

Jones closed the door. He held up his head and walked purposefully down the hall taking big steps. He turned into a room on his right. This too was over-full with gloomy furniture, making the room seem small and dismal. A grandfather clock ticked delectably in the corner.

The man made a flamboyant gesture with his arm to a comfortable-looking wing chair and Angel took it, while the other sat on a similar one at the opposite side of the highly polished fireplace, of which the black grate had not seen hot coal for many years.

Jones sat pouting in his chair, waiting for Angel to speak.

'You are Frank P. Jones, known as the Man in the Pink Suit?'

'If you say so,' he replied, drumming the arm of the chair with his fingers.

Angel peered closely across at him.

'No, sir. I don't say so. I am *asking* if you are?'

The man looked up at the ceiling, then shook his head slightly.

'Well then the answer would be yes, my name is Frank P. Jones, and sometimes I wear a pink suit,' he replied in a bored voice. 'I believe you knew that.'

'You were wearing the suit this morning?'

Jones frowned. 'Was I? I don't think I was, but if you say so. Does it matter?'

Angel's jaw tightened. 'You were seen wearing it.'

'Oh?' Jones raised his eyebrows. 'Amazing.'

There was a slight pause. Angel felt his pulse rate rising.

'Mr Jones, can I ask where you have been this morning?'

'You may.'

There was silence.

The two men looked at each other.

Jones was now tapping the tips of the fingers with their counterparts on the other hand while he alternately pursed and then relaxed his lips.

After a few seconds, Angel blew out a sigh. 'Well, where have you been this morning?' he demanded, angrily.

'Nowhere.'

'You were seen at a factory on the Northrop industrial estate.'

Jones shook his head. 'Really? What tosh? What would I be doing on an industrial estate?' he said with a sniff. 'I have been here all morning. I have not moved out of the house. I have no need to. All I want is within these four walls.'

'You were seen by four witnesses.'

Jones shook his head. 'They are wrong.'

'All four are wrong?'

'You said there were four. If it were four hundred and four they would still all be wrong. They were mistaken. Wrong. Seeing things. In error. Choose your own words.'

Angel shook his head. 'Are you saying you have been here all day?'

'Yes.'

'Was anybody here with you?'

'No.'

'You've not seen anybody all day?'

'No.'

'You've not had any visitors?'

'No.'

'Anybody phoned you?'

'Yes.'

'Ah. Who?'

'I don't know. I didn't answer it. It rang several times. It rings all the time. I don't always answer it.'

Angel licked his dry lips. 'So no one can corroborate your story that you have been in this house all day?'

'It isn't a story. I know that I have been here all day. It is my house. I have every right to be here. I don't need anybody to corroborate it.'

Angel shook his head and blew out a long sigh.

Jones frowned and leaned forward. 'Is this a game? Have I won something?' he asked, pertly.

'Won something?'

'Well it *is* some sort of contest, isn't it?'

'It most certainly is not.'

'Hmm. Well would you please tell me why my whereabouts this morning are of interest to you? I must say that you have captured my curiosity. I am utterly intrigued.'

'Do you know a man called Charles Tabor?'

'You haven't answered my question.'

'Do you know Charles Tabor?' Angel insisted.

'No. Should I?'

'He has a big factory on the Northrop Estate.'

He shook his head. 'I don't know people with big factories. And where they put them is of no interest to me.'

'Are you sure you don't know Charles Tabor?'

'I'm not good with names.'

'Tabor Industries make computers.'

'Oh yes,' Jones replied, pointing a finger upwards. 'Yes, yes, yes. Mmm. Charles Tabor. Horrible man. Yes I know *him*. I met him once.'

'You met him this morning.'

'No. No. I would have remembered. It would be a year or two back, now.'

Angel set his jaw. 'You went to his office this morning, in your pink suit with a gun and shot him.'

'In this weather? Don't be ridiculous.' He made a little

moue and then said, as an afterthought, 'But it's quite a good idea.'

'You deny it?'

'I do.'

Angel shook his head then he stood up. 'Where's the gun?'

The man smiled. 'The gun? Do I look like John Wayne?'

The inspector was not amused. He held out his hand. 'Where's the gun?'

Jones made an involuntary squeak of protest, shrugged and said:

'There is no gun.' Then he added: 'Is he dead?'

Angel looked at him sternly. 'Frank P. Jones, I am arresting you for the shooting of Charles Tabor. You are advised not to say anything, but anything you do say may be taken down and used in evidence. Do you understand that?'

Jones nodded and smiled knowingly.

'This is a ruse to get me to the studio, isn't it?'

'No sir. It isn't. This is very serious. You shot a man this morning in front of four witnesses. I am arresting you, and you're coming down to the police station.'

'I can't come now,' Jones said lifting his hands. 'I haven't had my lunch. And I have to finish a commentary on Rubens. I tell you what, you give me the address of the place and I promise I'll come down tomorrow afternoon. I should be finished by then.'

'No, sir. You have to come with me now.'

'Empty your pockets, sir.' Inspector Angel said.

Frank P. Jones looked all round the custody suite office.

'This really is the police station, isn't it?'

Angel looked at him in disbelief and shook his head.

'Come on, sir, empty your pockets.'

'Why?'

'For safety.'

'Safety? You said this was the police station. Isn't it safe here?'

'So that nothing goes missing. We list it and put it in this envelope. And sign for it. And that ring. Take it off. Do you have a watch?'

'Of course.'

'That as well, please.'

'Really. How will I know what time it is?'

Angel ran his tongue round the inside of his mouth.

'Where you are going, believe me, sir, time won't matter.'

Jones didn't seem to hear what was said. He was busy unloading his pockets of wallet, keys, handkerchief, some coins and a small bottle of pills.

Angel spotted the small brown plastic bottle with the white screw top and reached out for it.

'What are these for?'

'They're prescribed for me by my doctor,' Jones answered. 'I really need to have them with me.'

'What are they for?' Angel persisted still holding the bottle. He read the handwritten label: 28 Diazepam 5mg tablets. To be taken as prescribed by doctor. If sleepy do not drive/use machines. Avoid alcohol.

'If you must know, they're tranquillizers,' Jones said, his lips twitching.

'I know they're tranquillizers. They're Valium. What are you taking Valium for?'

Jones raised his head. 'It's nothing to do with you,' he said stubbornly.

'It's everything to do with me. I'm responsible for you while you're in here.'

'You're not a doctor.'

'What are you taking these for?' Angel persisted.

Jones looked up at the ceiling briefly. His face was white. He swallowed, licked his lips, then he snapped:

'They are to steady my nerves when I am appearing in front of the camera. Now, can I have them?'

'There are no television cameras in here. I'll just check them out with the doc,' Angel said, slipping them into his pocket. 'If he says it's all right, of course you can have them.'

'I really think you should let me have them now,' Jones said angrily.

'You won't need them in here.'

'Oh!' Jones growled angrily and turned away. 'Very well. Keep them. Keep them,' he snapped.

The door opened and DS Crisp rushed in.

'Hey sir. There's a tale going round the Station that you've arrested the Man in Pink.'

Frank P. Jones looked up and deliberately turned round to face the man. Crisp's jaw dropped.

'You have! It *is* him!'

Jones nodded and smiled like a benevolent dictator. Crisp stared and grinned back.

'Good afternoon, sir. I saw you on television on Saturday night.'

Jones maintained the smile, and nodded his head slightly at an angle, like royalty receiving the freedom of the city.

Angel's knuckles tightened. He dashed over to Crisp, grabbed him by a shoulder-pad and pulled him into a corner of the room. He spoke quietly through his teeth.

'Look here, lad. Are you out of your tiny mind? Get a grip on yourself. This is a police station, not *Blankety Blank*. There's no need for you to be fawning all over him simply because he works on the telly. This man is under arrest for attempted murder. Try and remember that.'

Crisp shrugged. 'I didn't mean anything, sir.'

Angel released his grip of the coat. He realized he might have overreacted.

'Yes, well, don't show yourself up, man. You're not a groupie. And he's not a god. He's only a man who works on the box, and gets overpaid for it.'

Crisp dusted down his coat and pulled it back into shape.

Angel returned to the desk, then turned round.

'I thought I told you to go to the hospital and keep an eye on Charles Tabor.'

'I did, sir. But his son was there and he was taken to theatre, and surrounded by doctors and nurses. I thought I was super-fluous.'

'What if I hadn't found Jones, and he had made a beeline for the hospital?'

'Well, er ...'

'Exactly.'

'Sorry, sir. I thought I could be more useful here.'

'In future, as long as you're on my team, Sergeant, note that I do the thinking. You do the doing! Right?'

'Yes sir.'

'Did you collect all those security tapes?'

'I put them on your desk, sir.'

'How many?'

'Four.'

'Right.' Angel sniffed. 'Look, he's been charged, and I've just started on his personal effects and valuables. You can finish off here. And when you have banged him away, go to his house. Dr Mac and his team will be there. Work behind them and see what you can find. *I want that gun.*'

'Right sir.'

They returned to Frank P. Jones.

The door suddenly opened and swung back noisily. Two young uniformed WPCs came in, talking and laughing. Angel glared across at them. The two women saw him. Their faces straightened.

'Oops! Sorry, sir.'

They stared at the man who was picking through the contents of his pockets on the desktop; their jaws dropped.

He looked at them, smiled quietly and for their amusement, and his own, dropped his keys and wallet on the counter with a flourish.

The women looked at each other, nodded and then giggled.

Angel's eyes flashed. He glared across at them.

'Get out!' he bawled.

The WPCs scurried away like schoolgirls at Hallowe'en and pulled the door close behind them.

Jones's eyes followed their exit. He smiled and then turned to Angel.

'You know, I really think they came to see *me*.'

Angel sniffed and turned away. 'You'll be wanting to contact your solicitor,' he said. 'If you give me his name, I'll arrange for him to visit you.'

Jones turned to face him.

'What for?'

Angel peered closely at him.

'What for?' he said slowly. 'Attempted murder, or wounding with intent to kill are very serious offences. You need all the help you can get!'

'Don't be ridiculous, man,' Jones puffed. 'Nobody in their right mind would believe I could harm a fly.'

Angel sighed. 'I have to say, Mr Jones, that unless you have evidence to the contrary, this case will go to court. The jury will nod like the front bench at Prime Minister's Question Time. And you will go to prison.'

'Poppycock!' Jones protested waggling a hand in the air.

Angel shook his head and pulled his chin into his chest.

'Well, that's the way it is, whether you believe it or not.'
Jones gave a disdainful snort.

'I can produce a thousand character witnesses.'

Angel shook his head. 'That won't make any difference. It doesn't work like that. I can produce four people who saw you pull the trigger. And you can't produce one to show you didn't.'

'I don't know what you mean,' Jones said. 'But I still don't need a solicitor. All this fuss! If this nonsense goes further, I would defend myself.'

Angel shook his head. 'Well, that's up to you. It's a very bad idea, sir, but it's up to you.' Then he asked quickly: 'What did you do with the gun?'

Jones frowned then turned slowly to face him. He put two fingers to his temple and closed his eyes.

'That was very devious of you, Mr Angel.' He opened his eyes and lowered his hand. 'I think you intended to catch me out. I have no gun. And I assure you, if I had a gun, I wouldn't know how to use it.'

Angel looked at him and shook his head. Jones raised up his head defiantly.

The Inspector turned to Crisp.

'Right, Sergeant,' he said quietly, ' I'm off. And don't you be long. I want you to go over the house before it gets dark. I want you to find that gun pronto.'

'Right, sir.'

Crisp carefully squeezed an inch of black ink from a tube on to a block in preparation to taking Jones's fingerprints. Angel looked over his shoulder.

'What are you doing now, lad? You don't need much of that ink. It's expensive. You're not blacking him up for *Showboat* you know.'

Jones's eyebrows shot up in alarm.

Crisp shook his head and began rolling out the ink.

The telephone rang. Angel crossed to a desk in the corner and picked up the receiver. 'Angel.'

After a moment, he sighed, pulled a face and said: 'Right, sir.'

He slowly replaced the phone and looked across at Jones, who was trying to remove the ring from his middle finger. He had his hands across his chest and his elbows were jigging about. His face was taut and the shaking caused a few strands of hair to fall across an eye.

'It's no good, man,' he protested to Crisp, who was patiently holding a big brown envelope. 'It won't come off. I've worn this ring for over twenty years. My mother gave me this when I left home to go to university. I've never taken it off.'

'Well leave it on then!' Angel bellowed.

Jones stopped struggling and looked across the room at the Inspector.

'What's that?'

Angel shook his head, slowly. 'If it won't come off, leave it on. Now you've got far more important things to worry about!'

Crisp and Jones sensed that Angel had something serious to say; they stared at him as he came towards them.

'The man's dead. It's now a case of murder,' he said coolly.

There was a pause.

Angel thought he noticed a slight smirk on Jones's lips. It soon left him when Crisp took one of his fingers and rolled it on the ink stone.

'What are you doing? What are you doing?' Jones said irritably.

'Relax your hand, sir. Just leave it to me. Relax!'

'I don't want that black stuff on my hands.'

'It'll soon wash off.'

'I hope so. I must have spotless hands. And clean nails. The camera picks up every little detail, you know. When I am holding a painting ...'

Angel closed the door of the custody suite and returned to his office, eager to view the security videotapes from Charles Tabor's factory. He had just sat down at his desk, when he heard the doorknob rattle and the door open. Superintendent Harker bustled into the room. He was carrying a sheet of paper.

'I've been looking all over for you, Mike.'

Angel stood up. 'I was in custody suite office, John.' It was unusual for the Super to come to his office. 'What is it?'

Harker breathed out hard. He shoved the paper at Angel.

'This fax has just come in.'

Angel read it:

From Bromersley General Hospital. 11.15 a m. 17.01.05.

Ambulance responded to anonymous triple nine call from phone-box on the Mawdsley Estate to unconscious man, aged about 45, covered in blood, found by children in stream under bridge off Canal Road. First aid administered in situ for abrasions and cuts to face, chest and abdomen. Admitted as an In Patient. Unable to establish patient's identity. Patient suffering from amnesia. Your attendance requested.'

'I have phoned the hospital,' said Harker. 'The doctor said it looked as if the man had been given a damned good thrashing by a rugby team. He is recovering well. They have no idea who he is. There's no identity on his clothes. He is conscious now, but doesn't have any recollection of what happened. Will you sort it?'

Angel nodded reluctantly and reached for his coat.

'I don't like that sort of thing happening on my patch, Mike.'

'No sir.'

Superintendent Harker swept out of the room and was away up the corridor as Angel turned the other way, walked past the cells to the rear door and the carpark. He reached the hospital in ten minutes. He asked at 'Enquiries' and found the mystery patient was in ward 36 on the fifth floor. He made for the lift and soon reached the ward. A young nurse with a squint was sitting at a small reception booth facing the entrance.

'Oh yes,' she said and referred to a crayoned chart on a board on the wall. 'We're calling him Miracle Man. He's in room 12. Down that corridor on the left.'

'How is he?'

She fingered through some notes. 'Doctor thinks he's very lucky. As far as he can tell, there are no vital organs damaged. Should be home in a few days. If he's asleep, don't wake him. He needs rest. And don't stay long,' she said bossily, slamming a folder back in the drawer.

Angel found the room and opened the door. Inside the little ward was a bed, a chair, a wash-sink and a locker. A man with a heavily bandaged head was asleep in the bed. Angel quietly closed the door, tiptoed across the room to the chair by the bed and sat down. He noticed that the man's feet almost touched the bottom rail of the bed and his head the top. The size of the blanket mound indicated that the patient possessed what the mail-order catalogues euphemistically refer to as the fuller figure. What could be seen of his face was red and blue and puffed up. He was bandaged round the temple and had a dressing on one cheek. He was lying on his back, his eyes closed, facing away from Angel and breathing evenly and noisily. He turned his head from side to side a couple of times, eventually resting facing the policeman.

Angel peered closely at him, and pondered for a moment. He thought he recognized him. He stood up and leaned over to have a closer look. Suddenly the man's eyes opened. He gasped and the bed shook as he saw a face so close to his. He pulled his hands out from under the blankets. Then he sighed when he saw who had been observing him so closely.

Angel smiled and sat down.

The man pulled a face and put his hands up to wipe the sleep out of his eyes and then winced as his fingers touched his swollen eyelids.

'Hurt, does it?' Angel grinned.

The man grunted. 'What you doing here?' he said.

'I've been told you'd had yours arms and legs torn off, they'd been stuffed in your mouth, choked you, that you'd died, and that the poor people you've cheated on the Mawdsley Estate were arranging to have a big party in the town hall to celebrate it,' said Angel. 'I've come to see if it's true.'

'Bah.'

'I see it isn't. Pity.'

The man growled and turned away.

There was a pause.

'The last time I heard about you was at Christmas,' Angel said. 'I heard you were in Strangeways, doing a roaring trade selling mistletoe to the poofters.'

The man snarled, and turned back to show an ugly selection of choppers.

'Go away.'

'How long have you been out?'

'A month.'

'Let out early, were you, on account of your impeccable charm and good looks.'

'Mmm.'

'And what're you calling yourself these days?'

'Eh? Same as always.'

Angel nodded. 'They told me you were pulling the loss-of-memory stunt.'

'Nah.'

Angel pointed to the thick white bandage wrapped all round his head.

'What's all this then? Are you changing your religion?'

The man swallowed and licked his dry swollen lips. 'Look here Inspector,' he said, 'can't you go and annoy somebody else? There's wards full of 'em out there. Hundreds of 'em. Why don't you visit them and ask *them* your daft questions?'

'You know, McCallister, you've got a mouth on you big enough to house a Black Maria. Ay, and a dog-patrol van as well. Why don't you try giving me some answers. What were you doing in that stream by Canal Road?'

McCallister pulled a face. 'I don't know.'

'You were hardly likely to be going swimming. It's only a foot deep. How did you get there?'

'I don't know. Have you got a fag on you?'

'I don't smoke. You ought to tell me how you got there, McCallister. It might save your life.'

The man shook his head and turned away to face the wall.

'What were you doing in the middle of January taking a swim?' Angel continued.

'I wasn't. I didn't. I don't know.'

'Somebody repaying a debt, was it?'

The man said nothing. He continued to look at the wall.

'Are you still working the same racket I sent you down for?'

'I'm not working no racket.'

'You mean you're not working, full stop.'

McAllister winced. 'Buzz off. I'm ill. I'm a patient. I don't have to put up with this,' he growled.

'Tut-tut, Tiny. Mind your temper. By the way, sorry about the bad news.'

McCallister's eyes flashed. He looked at him intently.

'Bad news? What bad news?'

'The doctor says you're going to be OK. You'll probably be home by the weekend. He thinks there are no vital organs damaged. That's bad news for all the poor souls on the Mawdsley Estate, your poor mother and me.'

'Oh.'

'Are you going to tell me what happened, then?'

'I fell down.'

'Is that the best you can do?'

'It's the truth.'

'What's happened to Spotty Minto?'

'Who?'

'Don't come 'who'. He got two years with you. And Irish John? Where's he now?'

'Don't know. Don't remember 'em.'

Angel sighed. 'All right, Tiny. You've got away with it this time. Next time you might not be so lucky. Whoever gave you this pasting might be back. And they might come back for you all tooled up.'

Tiny McCallister smiled, displaying teeth in glorious technicolor.

'Well, if they do, I'll be all ready for them, won't I.'

Angel shook his head slowly. He'd seen all this before. A crook escapes death by a hair's breadth and instead of learning how lucky he has been and making changes for his safety, displays nothing but bravado and engages in a programme of retaliation. He mistakenly thinks he's immortal. The result is a blood-bath, and innocent people get caught in the crossfire. Angel didn't want that on his patch!

'You think you're a big man, don't you,' Angel said. 'You

should wise up. Why don't you go down to the council, get a brush and get back to sweeping the streets like you used to do.'

McCallister leaned up on his elbows.

'Me, with a brush? Huh! Those days are 'istory. I would be mad to give up a good business. Don't you worry, Mr Angel. I can look after myself.'

The Inspector got to his feet.

'Oh yes? I'm sure you can,' he said sarcastically. Then he added thoughtfully: 'You know, you remind me of Toulouse Lautrec.'

The man's eyes opened wide. 'Eh? Who's he? Too Looze who?'

'Toulouse Lautrec. Look him up.'

'Never heard of him.'

'He was just like you.' Angel said heavily. 'Colourful. Handy with a brush. A connoisseur of food and drink. Especially drink. And very, very small.'

'Yah,' Tiny McCallister snarled.

'Yes,' Angel went on, 'And do you know what?'

McCallister turned to face him. 'What?'

'He died young, just like you are going to do.'

F O U R

When Inspector Angel left the hospital, he was not very happy with life. McCallister had not supplied any information that would be useful in catching his assailants, nor let slip any intelligence that might aid his investigations in other directions. All he had done was to waste Angel's time. He was therefore all the more eager to reach Bromersley police station to view the videos taken from Tabor's factory, and, he hoped, wrap up that murder and pass it to the CPS.

As he turned the street corner towards the prominent modern concrete-and-glass frontage of the station, he discovered he was running up towards an unexpected gathering of vans, cars and people. Two big vans with giant saucer-shaped aerials perched on their roofs were parked on yellow lines on the road in front of the station. One van was plain white, the other had the words IMPERIAL TV CHANNEL 44 in big red letters painted on the side. On the wide steps leading up to the double doors was a crowd of between twenty or thirty men and women, some standing with stepladders and cameras, some in jeans unloading connecting-boxes, mirrors and reflectors, and others rolling out wires. There were two tripods with larger cameras mounted on them. There were yellow and red cables from

the vans running in all directions. The centrepiece, positioned next to the main door was a tiny, blonde woman, who
was holding a microphone. She was stamping her feet and
blowing into her hands to warm them.

Angel was dumbfounded. He passed the circus and turned
into the station carpark. He approached the back door up the
now sand-covered slope where D S Gawber had recently
slipped and broken his ankle.

Two young men in jeans, jumpers and trainers, with their
hands in their pockets, were hovering at the bottom of the
slope. They peered at him superciliously as he passed.

He stopped, turned, and went back to them.

'What are you doing here?' he growled. 'What do you
want?'

'We're waiting,' one of the young men said. He touched his
mouth with a finger and gave a little sniff. 'Who are you?' he
asked defiantly.

Angel breathed in quickly and pulled in his stomach.

'What are you waiting for?' he said angrily. 'You're tres-
passing. Get out of it.'

The two young men looked at each other and smirked.

Angel glared at them. The skin on the back of his hands
tightened.

'*Move*! before I lock you up for loitering with intent,' he
bawled.

They hesitated, then the taller one said, 'We're waiting for
our boss.'

At that moment Angel heard the click of the bolt and the
back door opened. A constable rushed out and signalled to
Angel.

'The super wants you, sir. Urgently.'

'Right.' Angel waved towards the two young men. 'Who
are these?'

'They're waiting for the chap from the television, sir.'

'Eh? Oh. This isn't a stagedoor. Move them on, lad. Tell them to wait at the front of the station.'

Angel charged past the cells and up to Superintendent Harker's office. The door was open.

The superintendent was leaning against the front of his desk, remote control in hand, looking at a television set in the corner of the office. On the screen was an advertisement for a three-piece suite. His face was scarlet; his jaw set square. When he saw Angel, he turned off the sound and stood up.

'Ah!' he roared, pointing an arm and waving a finger at the end of it. 'Have you seen that lot in front of the station?'

'Yes. What's happened?'

The Super's eye caught the TV screen.

'Just a minute. It's the news. You are in for a shock. Listen to this lot.' He pressed the remote control. Loud booming music reverberated round the office.

Angel stood next to Harker with arms folded. They stared at the familiar picture of a newsreader in a dark suit and tie seated at a desk. The music faded. The man spoke:

'This is the news.

Frank P. Jones, the television personality known as 'the Man in the Pink Suit', was arrested this afternoon at his country home in Bromersley in South Yorkshire. It is alleged that he murdered Charles Tabor while the industrialist was working in his office. Charles Tabor was Chairman of Tabor Industries, the computer giant, which made a meteoric rise in its short life of two years. The accused, Frank Jones, who has just finished recording a new series, 'Man and Art,' is being held at Bromersley Police Station. We hope to bring you a live on-the-spot report from Anna Humphreys before the end of this bulletin.'

Superintendent Harker pressed the mute button and the TV went silent. He turned to Angel.

'They want somebody to make a statement. We must decide what to do. There's the TV boss man prancing up and down reception like an expectant father. He says if we don't give him an interview *now*, his boss will make him stay here until we do give him one. He needs a decision. He wants an officer – preferably you, as investigating officer – to give them a live statement in this newscast *now*.'

The phone rang. 'That'll be him again.' The super reached out for the handset. 'Harker … Yes. He's just come in. Hold on.' He turned to Angel. 'Yes. It's him. He needs an answer now.'

Angel didn't fancy himself as a television reporter, but the super obviously wanted him to give the statement. It would presumably defuse the situation, so what was there to lose.

'Yes. All right, John. Let's get shut of them.'

The Super nodded. 'Right,' he called down the phone, 'DI Angel will give you a statement. We're coming up now.'

He dropped the phone back in its cradle and went straight out into the corridor. Angel followed him. He tapped a number into the door lock and they entered the reception area.

The dozen men with cameras who had been in the waiting seats or lolling against the wall suddenly came to life. Camera lights flashed. Three policemen behind the counter jammed their heads through the enquiry window to see what was happening. A young man in denims and a blue jersey, wearing earphones and a microphone and carrying a clipboard and a mobile phone rushed up to the two policemen.

'Are you DI Angel?'

'Yes.'

'Will you come outside, sir? We are going live to London in two and half minutes. Excuse me, gentlemen. Excuse me.'

The photographers made a reluctant space for the trio to let them out of the building. The two policemen followed the floor manager through the door on to the steps outside. The small crowd outside surged nearer and the photographers pushed from behind. The young man positioned Angel next to the small blonde lady holding a microphone. She smiled at him. Angel instinctively closed his mouth and turned away at the powerful smell of Chanel. Another man clipped a tiny microphone to his tie and ran the wire along the floor to a connection box. Another man asked the policeman his name and title and chalked it crudely with a thick felt pen on a big card, which he then held above his head facing the woman. The man with the headphones was looking at a monitor, which was facing the young woman.

'Thirty seconds everybody!' he yelled suddenly.

The blonde lady turned to Angel, smiling.

'I'll simply ask you for a statement about the arrest of Mr Jones, Michael,' she said. 'Be as forthcoming as you can, will you?'

Angel nodded. 'Right. Yes.' He wasn't nervous. He had thought he would have been, but he would be glad when it was over.

'Louder please,' a voice from the van bellowed.

A big light on a stand was switched on.

Angel blinked. He wondered if his hair was in place. He reached up to his neck and pulled up his tie.

Another man tilted the lamp in all directions several times until a voice behind a camera said: 'That's it, Mark.'

A man appeared from nowhere with a card with the young woman's script on it. He held it up above his head.

'Is that all right, Anna?'

She read it. 'Yes. Fine.'

'Ten seconds.'

'Get that man to speak louder.'

The superintendent stood next to Angel but out of shot.

'Can you speak a little louder, Michael?' said Anna.

'Yes,' he bellowed. 'How's that?'

A voice from behind the crowd said: 'Thank you.'

Anna smiled. She seemed to be the calmest person there.

'Quiet everybody. Here we go!'

Suddenly somebody turned up a loudspeaker on a monitor. The newsreader's voiced boomed out.

'As reported at the top of the news, the man in the pink suit, Frank P. Jones was arrested on suspicion of murder today at his home in Bromersley. Our reporter, Anna Humphreys, is in South Yorkshire and takes up the story.'

The floor-manager pointed at the young woman. The loudspeaker went silent. Everybody froze. The bustle and yelling stopped. There was absolute stillness and silence. All that could be heard was the flapping of two pigeons overhead in the dull sky.

Anna Humphreys looked at the camera.

'I'm outside Bromersley Police Station where Frank P. Jones is being held,' she began. 'I am with Detective Inspector Michael Angel, who is in charge of the case.'

The camera lens zoomed back to give a two-shot.

Anna turned to him and said: 'Inspector, I understand you have Frank P. Jones under arrest. What is he charged with?'

Angel spoke with quiet calmness. 'The accused has been charged with the murder of Charles Tabor, a local man.'

'Can you tell us the circumstances of the murder?'

'Yes. He was shot in his office at close range at approximately eleven hundred hours today and died about an hour later.'

'What was the motive for the murder?'

'I'm not in a position to comment on that at this time.'

'Do you have any witnesses?'

'Yes, we do.'

'And what will happen now?'

'Well,' said Angel, 'he's been charged. The matter will go to the Crown Prosecution Service and thereafter I anticipate he will go to court and be tried before a jury.'

'Thank you.'

She turned back to the camera. It zoomed forward to a one shot of her.

'This is Anna Humphreys live at the Police Station, Bromersley, South Yorkshire.'

She remained in position holding the microphone for a few seconds until the man with the headphones yelled: 'Right. It's a wrap.'

She turned to Angel. 'Well, thank you, Michael. That was fine.'

The big light went out. The hubbub started again. Hands reached out and unclipped the wire from Angel's tie. Somebody else took Anna Humphrey's microphone from her and she moved away. A man lifted the camera off the tripod. The men holding the prompt-cards dropped them. Cables were unplugged from boxes and were being rolled up. All sorts of kit, reflector screens, monitors were being carried away down the steps and loaded in the vans.

Angel and the super turned towards the door. A gang of men in raincoats closed in on the two policemen, thrusting microphones and small recorders into their faces.

'Inspector, who were the witnesses? What do you think the motive was, then? Is the man in pink wearing the suit now? How long will he get? Will he get life imprisonment? When can we see him? Will he still be able to make his television programmes? Was there much blood? Can we speak to him? What does he say? Does he plead 'guilty'?'

Angel turned back. 'I'm sorry, gentlemen, there's nothing else I can tell you at this time. If you leave your cards at reception, I'll try to notify you if we have a press conference.'

'Is he allowed to have mail?' asked a man in a raincoat. 'If I left a note for him, would he be allowed to read it?'

'Of course. I must go,' Angel said.

'When's the press conference?' a man said.

'Where is it?' another man asked.

Without a word, the superintendent and the inspector pushed their way back through the station door. Two constables came out and good humouredly helped disentangle them from the crowd. Through the clamour, they made their way across the small reception area and through the security door. When Angel got it closed, he pushed against it to check it was locked, and then caught up with the Super. Together, hands in pockets, they ambled silently down the green corridor.

Superintendent Harker was the first to speak.

'The quicker we get rid of this case, the better. I can't do with time being taken up working round the media like this. I want you to push this one along, Mike.'

'I'll do what I can, John. It depends what comes up. You can't tell.'

'I haven't patience to see what comes up. Get shut of it,' he said brusquely.

'Right, sir.' There wasn't much else Angel could say to him. They walked on a few more steps.

'By the way,' Angel said. 'That man in hospital is Tiny McCallister.'

'McCallister? I remember him. A big lump of a man.'

'There's no amnesia. It was a punch up. A warning shot, I'd say.'

'Any idea who it might have been?'

Angel shook his head. 'They gave him a good pasting, but

they didn't want him dead. No heavy metal; some local godfa-
ther marking out his territory.'

'I don't like it. I don't like it one bit. I want every 'heavy' on
this patch with a record of violence visited and personally
warned by a senior officer.'

Angel sniffed. 'Where will I get time, John?'

'You can do *some* of them. The hardest. Let Gawber do the
rest.'

'He's off, with a broken ankle.'

'Oh yes. Set Crisp on then.'

'If you say so.'

'Well what else are we to do?' roared Harker.

'If we've time, John. We're always working against the
clock.'

'Do it,' Harker said tersely. 'I'll get out a list.'

Angel knew when not to argue. 'Right sir.'

He arrived at his office and turned into it. The super
continued down the corridor.

Angel's desk was just as he had left it when he had had to
chase over to Tabor Industries. It was littered with papers,
letters and reports. There were the four security videotapes in
the centre of the clutter. He expected them to provide conclusive evidence. He picked them up, trekked down to the CID
office and pushed one into the video player.

All four tapes had clear shots of the Man in the Pink Suit,
wearing sunglasses, hat, etcetera, exactly as he was seen on
television, even down to the suede shoes. Not much of his face
was distinctly visible, being obscured by the hat and
sunglasses, and there were very few moments when his face
was directly full front to the cameras. However, there were
clear, full-length pictures of him entering the reception area
of Tabor Industries, climbing the stairs, walking through the
general office and arriving in Tabor's office. He didn't touch

any of the internal doors. There was no need. They were all ajar. He didn't waste any time. As soon as he entered the office, Charles Tabor stood up. It looked as if he had shouted something. Two or three words, no more. The man in the pink suit instantly drew the gun out of his jacket pocket, pointed the gun at him and pulled the trigger. His aim was bad even though he was only a yard away from his victim. He seemed to have missed the heart and hit the stomach. Charles Tabor fell across the desk and slid behind it on to the floor. The fall was immediate and heavy.

It was like watching a Hollywood thirties gangster film. The fact that the tapes were played without sound made the scenes even more chilling. Then, without wasting a second, the man in the pink suit, waving the gun in his hand, retraced his steps through the general office and ran down the stairs to the reception area towards the outside door where he went out of shot of the camera.

Angel replayed the tape from the camera sited in Tabor's office several times in slow motion. The gun appeared to be an old fashioned Walther PPK/S. The man had pulled it out of his right hand jacket pocket and held it in his right hand throughout. Angel made a mental note to check whether Jones was right- or left-handed. It would add strength – not necessary, under the circumstances, but nevertheless helpful – to the case against him if it was confirmed that he *was* right-handed.

FIVE

Angel had had a very busy day and was pleased to reach home and relax. He didn't sleep well. He never did when he had a murder case to solve. He was only happy when he had accumulated all the relative facts, lined up the evidence, written his report and sent it across to the CPS. The following morning, he arrived at the office to find his desk in a mess. He buzzed Ahmed on the phone.

'You wanted me, sir?' the cadet said as he closed the office door.

Angel picked up a big handful of papers from his desk and waved them at him.

'What's all this stuff, lad?'

'They are letters, notes handed in and phone messages for the Man in the Pink Suit, sir.'

Angel sniffed. 'In this nick we call him Jones.'

'Right, sir, Jones. And there's a fair crowd of people in reception waiting to see him?'

Angel pulled an angry face.

'This is not a clinic, Ahmed. Reception isn't a waiting room. We don't do flu jabs. We've got to get reception sorted and kept sorted. We can't have people crowding round like a load of patients from the psychiatric ward,' Angel said, stuffing the messages into a large envelope.

Ahmed's eyes opened wide. 'What do you want me to do about it, sir?'

'*You* can't do anything, lad. Find DS Crisp and tell him to bring his Armani-clad backside in here.'

'Right, sir,' Ahmed said. He closed the door.

Angel took the envelope and a writing-pad and went down to the custody suite. The constable on duty let him into the cells area.

'Is Jones all right, lad?' Angel asked.

'Very subdued, I'd say, sir.'

'Is he any trouble?'

'No. He doesn't like the grub, but who does?'

Angel nodded knowingly. 'In a couple of minutes, will you bring us two teas? And I've a particular reason for asking you to bring them on one of those tin trays. And hand the tray to me.'

'Righto, sir.'

Angel nodded towards the cell door. The constable unlocked it.

Jones was on his bunk-bed reading a newspaper. He looked over his half-spectacles.

'Oh, it's you,' he said.

'It's me,' Angel said evenly.

Jones dropped the newspaper, stood up and faced Angel square on.

'I really must say that you should have allowed me to appear in that news programme on the television. It's not you they want to see on the screen, it's me.' He gave Angel a beady look. 'And they didn't show any photographs of me or any VT from my new series, I understand. Nothing! It just went on with this silly nonsense about Charles Tabor. All this use of my name and no mention of my new series, nor a penny in fees. That director should see my agent. He has all manner of tapes and stills of me including an up-to-date biography. Next time there is to be a news item concerning me, I want to know about it.'

Angel shook his head. He reached out for the chair by the door, sat astride it and put the big envelope on the floor.

'And while you are here,' Jones continued, 'I must say, this room is dreadful. I want an upgrade. If it costs more, I will gladly pay the difference.' He waved his arms in the air. 'It's primitive, stifling and very boring. And there's no view at all. There's nothing to look out onto. I don't know how long you intend keeping me in these conditions. I don't even know if it's legal. I need access to a phone. I need to phone my agent and my director. There may be others I need to contact. And I need some books. And my post will be piling up. And I may as well work on that Rubens programme while I am in here.'

Angel sighed. He failed utterly to understand the man.

'Haven't you got it into your head, Mr Jones, that you are in jail because you shot a man. You murdered a man. You may never walk free again!'

Jones blew out a puff of air. 'Poppycock! If you knew me, you'd know that I couldn't kill anything, not even a bluebottle. If one is buzzing around the window, I trap it in a glass tumbler and release it through the door.'

Angel shook his head. 'I have seen the videotapes. They prove the case against you.'

Jones looked up surprised. 'What videotapes? I'm not aware of any videotapes.'

'The security videotapes from Tabor's factory.'

'Oh!' Jones said, waving a hand irritably.

'Would you like to see them?'

'What for? Certainly not,' said Jones with a sniff.

Angel licked his lips. 'I thought it would give you some idea of the weight of the case we have against you.'

'Rubbish.' Jones waved a hand to indicate that he wished to close the subject.

Angel sighed. 'Let me ask you a question.'

'I've done nothing but answer your questions since you rang the bell on my front door yesterday,' said Jones, lifting his chin and looking down his nose.

'When you are on television and wearing your pink suit, sunglasses and so on, what shoes do you wear?'

'Shoes?'

Angel nodded.

'I have a pair of brown suede shoes that I keep especially for the occasion. I did try to get pink shoes. I went to Berman's. They didn't have any. My agent suggested that I had pair of black patent leather shoes painted, but I couldn't be sure of obtaining the right shade of pink. I did endeavour to complete the pink outfit but eventually decided that, as only the top half of me is usually seen, it didn't seem to matter that much. And those suede shoes are soft and comfortable and quite suitable for hanging around hot television studios and galleries.'

'How many pairs of suede shoes do you have?'

'Why? Just the one pair.'

The constable opened the door and proffered a tray with two mugs on it as arranged.

'Tea, sir.'

Angel took it and winked. 'Ta, lad.'

The cell door closed.

Angel turned and leaned forward to Jones with the tray.

'Help yourself.'

Jones stuck his nose in the air again.

'What is it?'

'Well, it's not champagne, lad.'

Jones frowned and looked at him sternly.

Angel wondered if he would take a mug.

Jones leaned forward and contemplated the two mugs. After a moment, he made a choice and took one.

Angel noted with satisfaction that he picked up the mug with his right hand. That was more evidence to confirm his guilt. He now wanted to see which hand he used when writing.

'You know, you really do need a solicitor,' he said heavily.

'Don't go on about it, man,' Jones replied, waving a hand in the air. 'Nobody in their right mind is going to believe that I could kill anybody, especially in that pseudo-dramatic way. It sounds more like a clip from an old James Cagney film.'

Angel ran his tongue round his mouth.

'Well, you weren't exactly a friend of Charles Tabor, were you?' he said cunningly.

Jones eyes flashed. 'Phh!' He held up a finger pointing to the ceiling. 'Horrible man. I was most certainly not. He was an unschooled, unprincipled money-grubbing thief and a liar. Anyone who has had any dealings with him will tell you that.'

'Oh?' Angel replied, trying to sound surprised.

Jones turned to the bunk and sat down. He took a sip of the tea, looked round for somewhere at table height to put the mug, and finding nowhere, settled for placing it on the floor.

'I'll tell you about that man, shall I?'

The policeman nodded, trying not to appear unduly interested.

'He had a tiny little shop selling office supplies; envelopes, paper, pens, pencils, that sort of stuff, on Sheffield Road before he suddenly branched out into making computers. About two years ago, I bought an office suite from him: desk, chair, stationery cupboard, filing-cabinet, you know the sort of thing, to set up a small office at home. He offered me a substantial discount if I paid in cash. It was tempting, so I agreed. It was duly delivered and I paid him personally two thousand pounds, in twenty-pound notes, I remember, on the worktop in my kitchen. Naturally, I thought that was the end of it. But he's been billing me for the stuff ever since. He says I haven't paid him. He has my signature for delivery and I haven't a receipt from him for payment, have I? Why, only the other day, I received a final demand, as they call it, from a firm of solicitors instructed by him. They are taking me to court next week. I think Charles Tabor thought I would be afraid of the bad publicity and would pay up to avoid it. He underrates me and he underrates the general public. The man is a fool. The public would believe me and not him, anyway.'

'The man is dead!' Angel said.

'Ha!' Jones eyes brightened as if he had only just heard about it. 'Revenge is sweet, saith the Lord.'

Angel shook his head. There it was. That was Frank P. Jones's motive for the murder of Charles Tabor: £2000. And the accused had admitted it, easily and openly. He had made no attempt to conceal the dispute and his dislike of the victim.

Angel reached down for the big envelope he had brought and held it out to Jones.

'There's some fan mail for you.'

Jones's eyebrows shot up. He smiled for the first time that day.

'Ooh.' He leaned over eagerly to take it.

'I'll want your signature,' said Angel. He pulled out his notebook and clicked his pen.

'Certainly.' Jones took the pen and scribbled something quickly.

Angel noted with satisfaction that he was writing with his right hand. That was all he needed from the man for the time being.

'There you are,' Jones said as he handed back the pad. He smiled knowingly. 'But I don't really have to sign for my post,

Mr Angel, do I? I don't know anything at all about police procedure, but I would doubt that.'

Angel didn't reply. He just looked across at him.

'You wanted my autograph and you didn't want to ask me for it,' Jones said, smiling and tapping the side of his nose with a finger. 'I know.'

Angel smiled weakly, shook his head and looked down at the pad. Jones had written: *Best wishes, Frank P. Jones.* Angel suddenly had a thought.

'Are you, by any chance, ambidextrous?'

The man was skimming enthusiastically through the forty or fifty letters he had taken out of the big envelope. Smiling, he glanced up at Angel.

'I say, all this in one day! What was that? Oh, am I ambidextrous? No, no, Mr Angel,' he said, holding up his right hand, shaking it from the wrist and waving it in the air. 'Just boringly normal.' Then he licked his lips, returned eagerly to the letters and muttered: 'Very normal, you know, very normal.'

Angel shook his head. He was far from normal. He watched Jones eagerly tear open an envelope, hurriedly read the contents, touch his lips, nod, smile, then throw the letter down and snatch up another. It was a fitting time to leave, Angel thought. Let him enjoy his fan-mail; after all, he wouldn't be luxuriating in the life of a celebrity much longer.

Angel returned to his office, dropped the notepad on his desk, slumped in the chair, leaned back on the headrest and closed his eyes. The evidence against Jones was conclusive. The statements made by the four eyewitnesses corresponded exactly with all the facts depicted on the tape. If DS Crisp was to phone him to say that he had found the gun somewhere in Jones's house, then that would indeed be the cherry on the cake. The case would be conclusive. It would have all the requirements of a classical investigation: motive, means and opportunity.

Nevertheless, he decided he would wait for confirmation from Dr Mac that everything was as straightforward as it seemed. There might be some supporting forensic evidence forthcoming. He had no doubt that the murder had been executed exactly as he had seen it. The man in the pink suit *had* murdered Charles Tabor in cold blood. For a change, he was giving the CPS the guilty party trussed up and bound. Even the cleverest of counsel couldn't cut through this evidence. You can't argue with facts. There was complete, consecutive videotape coverage of the Man in the Pink Suit, from the moment he stepped into the reception area, made his way up the stairs, through the general office into Charles Tabor's office, shot him, returned back through the general office and down the stairs to the reception area.

All the requirements of proof were there. Jones had no alibi. He said he was at home at the time of the murder, but he couldn't produce anyone who saw him there to confirm it. He hadn't answered the telephone or made a call that could have been checked on. He could easily have left his house by car, driven to Tabor Industries, shot Tabor and returned home, unnoticed. The whole business would have taken no more than twelve minutes.

The motive was clear. Jones had said that Charles Tabor had been trying to trick him out of £2,000, and that the court hearing was only five days away. If the case against Jones for trying to avoid paying a bill had gone ahead, it would not have done his public image any good. You can't argue with facts. There wasn't a jury in the world that wouldn't convict him. Angel brightened. He shrugged. The case was as tight as an elephant's pyjama cord.

The phone rang.

Angel leaned out for the handset. 'Angel.'

'It's Crisp, sir. I've found a gun.'

Angel pursed his lips. 'Great. Where was it?'

'In his car.'

Angel stood up. 'Was it hidden?'

'It was under the car seat, in the garage. Wrapped in a duster.'

'What sort is it, lad?'

'It's a Walther PPK/S.'

Angel felt his pulse rate increase. 'Sounds like the one. Are there any fingerprints on it?'

'It's been wiped clean, sir.'

'Hmm. Is Dr Mac there?'

'Yes, sir.'

'Put him on.'

The doctor coughed as he took the phone.

'Yes Mike?'

'Mac, will there be any evidence from that Walther PPK/S to show who fired it?'

'No. But the registration number is still partly decipherable. It has been attacked by a banshee with a rat tail file, but we might still get a lead.'

Angel's eyebrows lifted. 'Ah. That's something. Hmmm. Will you let me have confirmation as to whether that is the gun that killed Charles Tabor?'

'Of course.'

'Right. Jones was wearing his stage clothes, pink suit, pink shirt and so on at the time of the shooting.'

'We've got all those. They are altogether in a smart leather suitcase.'

'Good. He was wearing a pair of brown suede shoes.'

'Right.'

'He says there's only the one pair.'

'We'll find them.'

'And have you seen a pink carnation anywhere?'

'Aye. In the rubbish bin.'

'I'd like to see it.'

'I'll bring it for you to see.'

'Thanks Mac. 'Bye.'

Angel replaced the phone, leaned back in the chair and closed his eyes briefly. He was thinking that Jones would have presented himself at Tabor's factory exactly as he would have been seen if he had been appearing on television, even down to the flower in his buttonhole. He was probably wearing make-up as well!

Another thing. There'd been no identification parade. He wondered if the defence would insist on it. The judge would have to allow it. The CPS would probably advise it, before the case reached court. That would require nine pink outfits! There was no other way to do it. What a farce. One pink suit is bad enough, but nine pinkos all lined up. It would look like a pier show. Never mind. It was all in the name of justice.

The phone rang. He reached out.

'Angel.'

'There's a Mark Tabor on the line, sir.'

'Right. Put him through.'

'Inspector Angel?' the young man said breathlessly.

The policeman sensed that something else was wrong. 'Yes, Mr Tabor.'

'I want to report a robbery.'

Angel's car reached the hatched area outside the front door of Tabor Industries in a record six minutes. He slammed on the brakes, dashed through the automatic doors, ran up the steps, along the landing and into the front office. Mark Tabor was alone, in his shirtsleeves seated at his late father's desk, holding his head in his hands.

He looked up as Angel walked in.

'There is about one hundred and five thousand pounds missing, Inspector. How am I to replace that?' he wailed. 'Some of that cash was for the wages. They are due to be paid on Friday.'

'Where was it stolen from?'

'I'll show you.' Mark Tabor pushed back the swivel chair and swiftly slipped round the desk to the Chinese cabinet in the corner of the room. The black-lacquered door and the heavy safe door inside it were wide open. The safe was empty apart from several dusty envelopes wrapped in pink tape in a corner at the bottom. He held out both hands, pointed towards it and said: 'In there!'

Angel looked briefly at the empty safe.

Mark Tabor shook his head, returned to the desk and sat down.

'And it was locked,' he continued. 'It's been locked all night. It takes two long keys to open it. They go deep into the casing of the safe. And the alarm was on. There is a special magnetic switch across both locks. You wouldn't get a key or anything else metal near it when the alarm was set. And there's no way it can be opened without the keys.'

'And where are they kept?'

Mark Tabor picked up and waved two keys with shafts twelve inches long from the desk.

'Dad kept them on the desk, while he was here, but he would always take them with him whenever he left the office.'

'Have they been here all night?'

'Oh no. I took them home with me,' Mark Tabor said quickly. 'But they would have been on the desk yesterday, when Dad was shot. They would still have been here when your men were here yesterday and during the time I was at the hospital. They would have been here all the afternoon until I returned. That would have been about five o'clock. They were still on the desk. They were covered in fingerprint powder. When I left for home, I picked them up and took them with me.'

'So the keys were unattended between the time my men left, which was about four o'clock and the time you got back from the hospital?'

'I suppose so.'

Angel looked up at the CCTV camera directed at the desk.

'Won't the videotape tell us anything?'

Mark Tabor ran a hand through his hair.

'The tapes were taken out for your sergeant to take away. We haven't any replacements. They run for twenty-four hours on a continuous loop system. Oh dear!' he groaned. 'That's something else I'll have to see to.'

'Who would have access? To this office and the safe, between four and five o'clock yesterday afternoon?'

'As news filtered down to the assembly line, production ground to a halt,' said Mark. 'There were apparently discussions among the staff. The shop-floor was in some confusion. During that time, anyone could have come up here without being missed, I expect. I suppose the four girls in the general office and the receptionist might have seen anybody who shouldn't have been here, but they left early.'

'Anybody else?'

'I suppose it could have been anyone or a group of people – employees – who had the nerve and who knew that there was a worthwhile amount of money in the safe.'

'They would have needed to know about the safe keys. That they were on the desk.'

Mark Tabor nodded

'And you are sure the money was in there at the time your father was shot?'

'It must have been. I had brought a hundred thousand

pounds from the bank yesterday morning. So much happened yesterday. It must have been. Could Jones have stolen it? Perhaps that's what he came for.'

'No. That's one chap we can eliminate. It would have shown up on the tapes. Why was there so much cash on hand?'

'Dad had said he had a big deal coming up. He always used to say that he could negotiate better with cash. Don't know what it was.'

'Will your father's secretary know? What's her name?'

'Ingrid Dooley.'

'Ay, will she be able to throw any light on this?'

Mark shrugged. 'I don't know. She couldn't tell *me* anything. I'll get her.' He crossed to the door, opened it and called: 'Ingrid.'

Miss Dooley glided in. She was as pretty as yesterday although Angel had then no time to notice. She stood by her office door, soberly dressed in a tight black dress. She flashed her big, brown eyes across at the policeman and smiled briefly.

'Good afternoon, Miss Dooley. Can you help us? A brief question. Where were you yesterday afternoon?'

Her moist lips smiled. 'After you interviewed me, I went out for a walk. I needed some fresh air. You took over my office and I needed to go somewhere, away from all this for a while.'

'Yes, of course. Where did you go?'

'Nowhere particularly. Just round the estate.'

'What time did you get back?'

'About five o'clock, I suppose.'

'That's right, Inspector,' said Mark Tabor. 'Ingrid got back just after I did.'

'During the few days leading up to, and indeed on the day

of the murder did you see anybody hanging around this office at any time? Anyone who shouldn't have been here?'

'No, Inspector.'

Angel nodded. 'We believe there is a lot of money missing from the safe, Miss Dooley. I wonder if you can help us?'

She touched her lips with the tip of her tongue, then said: 'Yes, Inspector. Mark's already told me.'

'Do you know how much there was?'

She shook her head. 'Mr Tabor dealt with the money himself. I never had anything to do with it.'

Mark looked up from the desk.

'That's right, Ingrid, but there was usually a lot in there, wasn't there,' he said nervously. 'Tell the Inspector.'

'Oh? Yes. There was.'

'But you have no idea how much?'

Ingrid hesitated and looked across at Mark Tabor.

'It's all right. Tell him, Ingrid,' he urged.

She shrugged, then said: 'Well I don't know exactly, but well over a hundred thousand pounds.'

Angel puckered up his lips and made a silent whistle. He saw Ingrid look at Mark, who nodded approvingly.

Angel rubbed his chin.

'Why did he need that sort of cash on hand?' he asked.

'There was the wages, and the petty cash.'

'Petty cash?' Angel's eyes opened wide.

Ingrid Dooley's mouth tightened briefly and then relaxed. She looked away.

There was a sudden clatter of metal hitting metal and a thud.

Angel turned to find out the cause of the noise.

'I'm sorry. It was me. I am all fingers and thumbs,' Mark Tabor said, as he bent down and picked up the safe keys from the carpet and put them back on the desk.

Angel had been fully engaged watching the dimple on Ingrid Dooley's cheek form and then vanish as she answered his questions and had not been aware that Mark had been fidgeting with the keys.

Tabor ran his hand through his hair.

'Excuse me, Inspector,' he said. 'I really must get on.' He reached over the desk and picked up the phone. 'I have to try the bank for a loan.'

Angel looked from one to the other.

'There appears to be nothing more I can do about it at the moment. But I'll certainly look into it. Now, if there's nothing else, I must go.'

S I X

Angel stopped his car outside the little shop on the Mawdsley Estate. Two fourteen-year-old boys with hair sticking out in all directions, wearing jeans purposely torn at the knees, were leaning against the shop window. They had their hands in their pockets and were conspicuously looking nowhere. They couldn't speak, either, because their cheeks were bulging as their mouths opened and closed unpleasantly in a puzzling, laboured, rhythmical time. It was impossible to determine what they were chewing, but it was red, luminous and would have served well as a tail-light on a 707.

They eyed Angel suspiciously as he walked across the concrete space, which had once been a patch of grass, to the shop door, accidentally kicking an empty lager-can that was in his path. The door was wide open and propped back by a flat-iron, which was on a handmade rug made from scraps of old clothes. The shop was the converted sitting-room of a terraced house and was stuffed to the ceiling with every kind of food and drink, enough to feed the Eighth Army. It was so crammed that there was only enough floor-space to allow three small customers inside the premises at a time.

Fortunately for Angel, nobody was requiring the shop-keeper's attention as he stepped down into the room. He was not surprised to see the heavy woman behind the brightly illuminated glass counter. She wore a woollen cardigan, a headscarf banded her hair, and she had gold rings on every finger. She was the centre of the congestion and the creator of it.

'Good morning, Kathleen. Can I see Irish John?' Angel asked equably.

She was squeezing loaves of bread from a baker's tray into shelves improvised from packing cases set on their sides. She blinked at the sight of the policeman and opened a mouth big enough to bite off a Catholic's head. 'Naw. He doesn't larve here onymore,' she hollered in a peaty Belfast accent.

She returned to stacking the bread.

Almost immediately, the head of a man with a face like a ferret appeared slowly round the door-jamb behind the woman. Seeing the inspector it swiftly slid back.

Angel spotted him.

'Hey, John. I want you,' he called.

There was a three second delay and the head slowly reappeared.

Kathleen saw him. She turned back to Angel. 'Glory be. He's retorned. It's a miracle,' she exclaimed without any emotion.

Irish John squeezed up to the counter and stood next to Kathleen. He was a tall, skinny man with a small head. He had a white scarf round his neck and was wearing a trilby that didn't need any further camouflage. He looked pleased with life and smiled slightly. He had a very thin cigarette between his brown stained fingers. It gave off blue smoke and a strange smell.

'Well now, it's Inspector Angel,' he said slowly. 'Now what would you be wanting me for now?' He took a small drag from the spindly cigarette.

Kathleen turned quickly and deliberately caught him on the ear with a loaf of bread.

CHAPTER SIX

'There's no room for the boath of us behind this counter, John. Oive told you that before, I have. And there's no smoking about the food.'

A little woman came into the shop and rammed a pushchair into the back of Angel's legs. He turned round to see what was happening. The little woman looked up at him.

'Are you being served, mester?' Before he could reply, she called out: 'Kathleen, I want a bottle of vinegar and twenty ciggies.' Then she held out her hand to Angel and said, 'Here. Give her this. I can't get round you.'

Angel declined the money.

'If you back off with that pushchair, you can come up to the counter.'

She didn't move.

Angel glanced back. John had gone and Kathleen's big, podgy face glared across the room at him.

'Where is he?' asked Angel.

'He'll be out the bark,' she said loudly and pointed a banana-sized finger to the shop door. 'Outside and up the ginnel.'

Angel made a mighty stride over the pushchair. A child's face with chocolate round its lips and cheeks, and big eyes, looked up in amazement at him. The policeman managed to untangle himself from the pushchair and stepped out through the open door. The little woman leaned back against the wall, folded her arms, stared at him and sniffed.

He turned immediately right and then right again up a passageway in the terrace block. It led to the backyard of the shop. It was an untidy patch of overgrown grass and weeds. He turned to the back door and tapped on it. It was immediately opened by a boy aged eight years.

'Are you a capper? 'Cos moy Dad don't live here onymore,' the lad said in an accent learned at his mother's ample knee.

Before Angel could respond, the door opened wide and there stood Irish John. The little boy scurried round his legs into the house.

The man was still smiling. His head was shaking a little and he still had the spindly cigarette dangling between his fingers. He hung on to the door as if it needed his support.

'You wanted me, Mr Angel, did you now?'

'Just calling round to see how you're getting along, John.'

John smiled. 'Oh? I didn't know you was running a benevolent soarvice for ex-prisoners,' he said slowly.

Although he spoke in a light-hearted way, Angel knew there was a deep-seated potential malevolence in every word.

'You've been out about two months now haven't you?'

'Yes,' said John, taking a pull at the cigarette, blowing out the smoke and licking his lips with a blue tongue. 'And I haven't had a visit from the local fuzz. Where've you all been? I was beginning to feel neglected, Mr Angel. It's as if you weren't interested in me onymore.'

'You're not the only villain on the patch you know.'

'Oh? Is that right?' John took a drag from the spindly cigarette and produced another cloud of blue smoke and a peculiar smell.

'There's your mate, Tiny McCallister. For instance.'

'Never hoard of him, I haven't.'

Angel gave him an old-fashioned look.

'You went down with him for two years for extortion with menaces. You've had the doubtful pleasure of his company at Strangeways during that time. There were three of you. You, him and Spotty Minto. The three stooges. Where is Spotty, by the way?'

'Never hoard of him. That I haven't.'

Angel rubbed his hand across his chin. He made a disagreeable face.

84

'I haven't patience to talk to you,' he said angrily. 'I'll find him. You can be sure of that.'

Irish John smiled. 'Now you've found me, Inspector, what is it you're wanting?'

Angel pulled himself to his full height and stabbed a finger into the lapel of Irish John's navy-blue jacket.

'I've come round to tell you to keep your nose clean. You will, no doubt, know that your friend McCallister has taken a beating. So if you're thinking of retaliating on his behalf, do it in Leeds or Manchester or somewhere else, because I won't tolerate it here. Do you understand?'

Irish John raised his eyebrows. The smile had disappeared. His mouth opened and stayed open.

'We are watching you,' Angel continued, 'and you can tell your mates. One sign of trouble – from you or them – and you'll go down for five years. I'll see to it personally.'

'You've got nuthin' on me, Inspector,' said John slowly in a sing-song voice.

Angel looked down at the spindly cigarette.

'I could book you right now for possession of cannabis.'

John's jaw dropped. He glanced down at the fag and then put it behind his back. He hesitated and then said:

'It's proscribed for me by a doctor.' He nodded slowly for emphasis. 'I have to have it. It's for my illness.'

'What illness,' Angel snapped.

Irish John rubbed his chin with four fingers and a thumb.

'Erm. I forget.'

'You forget? Well don't forget what I've told you. Keep out of trouble.' Angel turned to go.

'Er – Mr Angel,' Irish John called.

The policeman turned back. 'What now?' he growled.

'I've remembered.'

'What?'

'I've remembered what it is I had forgotten ... what I have the stuff for,' he said slowly.

'Oh? What?'

'My memory.'

Angel glared at him. 'Oh?'

'Yes. So you see it was no surprise was it, that I had forgotten. Indeed, I have a lot of things the psychiatrist in Strangeways said I *should* forget. Things from when I was a child in County Cork. The potato-famine, the troubles, the unemployment, the poverty, being an orphan, and my father who was always drunk. It was terrible.'

John shook his head and looked down.

Angel took a step back from him.

'What *are* you talking about? *You* don't come from Ireland. As far as I know, you've never been to Ireland. Your record says you were born in Glasgow. And you weren't an orphan either. Your father was a very stupid conman and thief. Your mother was from a very well-regarded family. She was a qualified chemist. Your maternal grandparents were very respectable people. Your grandfather was a member of the Salvation Army and was teetotal. You lived with them and your mother. You ran away from them when you were fourteen to join a gang of shoplifters. You got caught and put on probation. The court delivered you back home and your mother was pleased to have you back – I don't know why. But you didn't stay long. You defied a court order saying you had to live at home until you were eighteen. A few months and you were off again, in spite of pleadings from her and her parents, and you've been in and out of remand homes and prisons ever since. You had endless 'second chances'. You came to live in Bromersley about ten years ago and you've been a damned nuisance to all and sundry here ever since.'

Irish John stood with his mouth wide open.

'That's not true, Mr Angel. I was in Belfast in 1994,' he said indignantly.

'Were you? Were you on a day-trip?'

'I was there for tree months. *Tree* months! I met Kathleen and her mother there. So what you say is not true. And what's more, I've married her. An Irishwoman. Kathleen Docherty. That's proof. You've met her. That's our son, Liam.'

'You're not married.'

Irish John hesitated.

'Well, we're going to be,' he stammered.

'Going to be – doesn't mean you are!'

Irish John pouted. 'There you are disputing all that I say,' he whined. 'Trying to make out I am telling lies.'

Angel came up to him. He shook his head. 'You *are* telling lies,' he said. 'You're stupid, John, stupid. You're like a bungalow. You've only got one story, you're low down, and there's not a lot going on upstairs!'

Angel returned to his office at the police station. His desk was covered with paper in one form or another, mostly letters. His in-tray was piled more than ten inches high with unopened envelopes in all sizes, colours and descriptions, mostly bearing UK postmarks, some with foreign stamps, some typewritten, mostly handwritten, almost all addressed to the Man in the Pink Suit or Frank P. Jones. Angel sorted through them, envelope after envelope. He put letters and papers for his attention on his left and mail for Jones in the in-tray until it grew more than ten inches high. The pile toppled over, some letters fell on to the floor. He scrambled down to pick them up and blew out a long sigh as he packed them safely in the tray. Then he leaned back in the chair, stared at the ceiling briefly and closed his eyes. He found it difficult to understand why a man like Jones should receive so much fan-mail. The man wasn't even good-looking. He'd less charm than a fridge. This was 'celebrity worship' gone mad. All the man seemed to know about was art and artists. He was no Don Juan. Angel's mind wandered down a few dead ends and then he heard a distant church clock chime. He opened his eyes, looked at his watch, tipped the chair forward and reached out for the phone.

'Ahmed?' he called down the mouthpiece.

'Yes sir.'

'Come in here, lad.'

Angel slammed down the phone, leaned back in the chair and rubbed his hand over his chin. A minute later Ahmed knocked at the door.

'Come in, lad.' Angel pointed to the wire tray heaped with letters. 'Take that lot to that chap in the cells.'

Ahmed grinned, flashing his even white teeth.

'The Man in the Pink Suit? Yes sir,' he said enthusiastically.

'In this nick we call him Jones,' Angel said sourly.

The grin disappeared. 'Yes sir,' Cadet Ahmed Ahaz said with a straight face. He picked up the wire tray and turned to go.

Angel had a thought.

'Ahmed. Can you operate that new videotape editing clobber?'

'Yes sir.'

Angel picked up the four tapes and held them in his hand while he spoke.

'Well, copy all these four tapes, and then, from the copies, edit the tapes tightly to show Jones appearing in the reception area, his progress up the stairs through the general office, into Tabor's office, the shooting, then his return through the office and back down the stairs. The sequence should only run for about ninety seconds. You'll see what I mean.'

'Right sir.'

Angel dumped the four tapes into the basket on top of the heap of mail.

There was a knock on the door and it swung open. There came a familiar voice.

'Are you free, Mike?"

'Come in, Mac. Nice to see you.' Then to Ahmed, Angel said: 'Off you go lad. That editing job is urgent. Do it next.'

Ahmed struggled to the door with the wire basket. He brushed past the Scotsman.

'Excuse me, sir.'

'It's all right, laddie. I'll get the door after ye.'

Angel stood up. 'To what do we owe the pleasure of your company?'

Mac closed the door behind the cadet and came up to the inspector.

'I have a result on the gun.'

Angel look intently at him. This vital news could put Jones away for life. He licked his lips.

'What?'

'We did the field tests this morning. It's positive. It *is* the gun that killed Charles Tabor.'

Angel slowly nodded. 'Right.'

'Ay. But the number on the gun is difficult. Some of the digits have been partly obliterated. I don't know if we'll be able to make it out. It will be interesting to see if it can be traced back to him. I've a lad working on it now.'

'Soon as you can, Mac.'

'Ay.'

Angel heaved a sigh. 'What makes a dandy man like Jones choose a small, vicious piece like a Walther?'

'The PPK/S .32 automatic is small. Fits in the pocket. Cuts anybody down at close range.'

'He must have hated Charles Tabor.'

'Incidentally, the clip still had seven rounds in it. So it had been fully loaded. I suppose he might have spent more rounds if anybody had got in his way while he was making his escape.'

'I don't like guns. I'm glad to have it off the streets,' Angel said, pulling a face. 'Have you gone over his clothes yet?'

'Should have that for you in a couple of days,' answered the doctor as he pulled a sealed see-through packet out of his pocket. It contained a pink carnation. It was drooping, but far from dead. He dropped it on the desk in front of Angel.

'You wanted to see that?'

'Ay.' Angel picked it up. 'Only to see whether it could have been worn yesterday morning or not, that's all.' He looked at it closely. 'What do you think?'

'Oh, it was. There are the slightest grey marks of powder burns on the flower itself and two minuscule specks of blood on a petal. I expect to get a positive reading that the blood is Tabor's, but we'll see.'

'Hmmm. Right.' Angel tossed it thoughtfully back on the desk. 'If only it could talk.'

'And I've got this for you. Might be something. Might be nothing,' the wily Scotsman said, waving a small key and a key ring at him. Angel took it and looked at it closely. The key was small, flat, made of white-metal, one and three-quarter inches long. It had the letters LF and the word England stamped on one side, and a number, 92283, on the other. It was suspended from a plastic key-ring, the sort of thing businesses give away for advertising purposes. It was a small, flat, six-sided plastic moulding in the form of a television set, and it had the words 'Imperial TV Channel 44' in blue on white and the station's logo: a television mast with rays drawn on it to suggest transmission.

'One of my lads found it between two flagstones in the back

garden. Well, it's not a garden. He's got the whole area flagged over. In the backyard. Do you ken, that house has not a blade of grass in sight. That man's a heathen. Very unnatural.'

'I know. Was it hidden?'

'Don't know.'

'And what do you think the key is from?'

'I don't know. We tried the burglar alarm, a filing cabinet and the locks on the double glazed windows. It wasn't for any of them. I don't know what else it might fit. I reckon it could be a safe-deposit box in a bank somewhere.'

Angel's eyes glowed briefly. 'I'll ask him. I'll see if he'll tell us,' he said, pocketing the key. Then suddenly he added: 'I knew there was something.' He began searching around in his coat pocket. He produced the little bottle and held it out. 'I've got these pills. They were in Jones's possession.'

Dr Mac took the container and read the label.

'Yes? Hm. 28 Diazepam 5mg. Yes?'

'I wondered if it would be safe for him to have them, I mean while he is in custody. He says they were prescribed for him by his doctor. He says they are to help his nerves when he does his stuff on the telly. What do you think?'

'Sounds reasonable.'

'Should I let him have them?'

'Depends on his temperament really.'

'What do you mean?'

'Well if he can be trusted to take them as directed, it would be all right.'

'I don't know that, do I?'

'Well, they're a common tranquillizer; they're obviously dangerous if misused. And diazepam is a hypnotic. Very useful to someone who's doing *his* job, I should think. But they're addictive.'

Angel's eyebrows shot up. '*Hypnotic?*'

Dr Mac unscrewed the white cap and shook one of the pills into his palm.

'Yes. They look all right. Yes.' He looked up at him. 'A hypnotic drug induces tranquillity, sleep.'

'What has it to do with hypnosis then?'

'Well, hypnosis *is* sleep: controlled superficial sleep.'

'Does a hypnotist or a hypnotherapist use a hypnotic drug to put his patients under, then?'

'Not necessarily. He might use it as an aid.'

'Oh?' said Angel. 'I didn't know that. And don't they say if a subject had been hypnotized once, he'll be an easier subject for hypnotic suggestion on any subsequent occasion?'

'What are you getting at?'

Angel hesitated. 'Well, do you think Jones could have been hypnotized?'

Mac rubbed his chin. 'I don't know, Mike. Why do you ask that?'

Angel pointed to the chair opposite him.

'Sit down a minute.'

Mac sat down and Angel swivelled his chair to face the doctor. He wiped a hand across his mouth.

Dr Mac sighed.

'It's possible,' he said. He licked his lips and his eyes narrowed as he considered the question further. Then he shook his head. 'But a man in a trance wouldn't do anything that was contrary to his natural instinct.'

Angel leaned further forward over the desk.

'He hated the sight of Charles Tabor!'

'Hmmm. Well, I suppose I've got to admit it's possible.'

'Come in!' Superintendent Harker bawled.

Angel opened the super's door. The eyes in the turnip-shaped head were already staring at him.

'You wanted me, John?'

'I do,' said Harker crisply and pointed at a chair.

Angel sensed something was wrong.

'What's up?'

The grey-haired man threw his pen on to the desk.

'Have you noticed anything unusual about this nick, Mike?'

Angel thought for a moment. He wondered what the super was referring to.

'No sir.'

'Well, I'll tell you. Have you not noticed that there are thirty-odd press men, two television vans, innumerable cars and, now that the holidays are with us, a gang of twenty or thirty star-struck kids on skateboards banging up and down the front steps of this police station? Have you not noticed that the reception area is now in a state of permanent siege? There are four men with cameras occupying the bench-seat intended for three, dropping chewing-gum and newspapers, knocking hell out of our tea machine and earwigging our everyday business.

'It is so busy out there, I now have to have an additional officer on duty round the clock. The switchboard is fielding upwards of a hundred phone calls a day from the world's press as well as the general public asking the most inane questions. And the number increases as the days go by. They are asking, will the man in pink be hanged? Where can they see the execution? Is it true he's on hunger strike? Is it true he has had both his hands cut off? What does he eat? Is there anything he needs? And from teenage girls and old women, 'Will you tell him that Ermintrude from Salt Lake City will marry him whatever he's done.' A chap from Hollywood wants to fly over to see him. Can it be arranged to meet him? He says his story will make a great movie. And so it goes on.

'The Chief Constable is getting tired of this nuisance, and

so am I. Let's get this poofball out of this station, into court and on remand. Let somebody else … let Armley put up with this pantomime!'

Angel felt his pulse notch up twenty beats and his face burn with anger.

'I don't like it either. What can we do about it?'

'I'll tell you what we can do about it,' Harker replied, his powerful jaw set square and his blue eyes glowing like Ferrari headlamps. 'Get Jones in court. Get him on remand. And get rid of this entourage and all this unwelcome nuisance. What more do you want? I understand that you have four eyewitnesses, critical videotape and now the gun found in his car. Added together it makes a rock solid case, doesn't it.'

'I haven't got all Mac's reports in yet. I've no forensic on his house, his car or the clothes he was wearing.'

'I think you're just stalling.'

'And I have not found out where the big wad of money reported missing from Tabor's safe around the time of his death has gone to, either.'

'Has that anything to do with Jones? Are you thinking Jones did it or had a hand in it?'

'I don't know. *I don't know*! He couldn't have stolen it at the time of the shooting, anyway. It would have shown on the tape. But nevertheless, it's still missing!'

'Well in that case, tackle it separately. You have nothing to link it to Jones. Jones isn't known to be a thief or short of funds, is he?'

'No.'

'Well, what more do you want? I want to know what the delay is. I *had* thought you had the case all sewn up. Isn't it ready for the CPS yet?'

'Confirmation. A few loose ends, John. That's all.'

'Oh? What? We haven't time for any finesse, you know.'

'A few inconsistencies then,' Angel added by way of explanation.

'Like what?'

Angel rubbed his earlobe between his first finger and
thumb.

'Well, I can't make my mind up why the crime was executed
by the man wearing clothes that were, after all, his personal
trademark: a bright pink suit. You don't see a lot of those
about, do you. In fact, you don't see too many murders
committed in broad daylight in front of witnesses either. It's as
if Jones wanted to advertise the fact that it was *him*.'

'You're getting fussy, man. Who gives a toss why he chose
to commit the crime in his party suit? It would have made no
difference to me if he'd shot the man in his birthday suit! Let's
be thankful we've got eye witnesses, CCTV and the gun.
What else do you need?'

'Mac suggested that maybe he was ill, suffering from
amnesia, shock or even that he might have been hypnotized.'

'Rubbish!' shouted Harker so stridently that his false teeth
nearly bounced out on to the desk.

Angel's tongue rolled round his mouth before he said:

'I wouldn't want us embarrassed in court.'

'Let the CPS worry about that.'

Angel sighed.

'They wouldn't proceed if they thought the case was too
weak,' the super continued. 'They'd be back to us for more
evidence. Now, is there any other reason why we shouldn't
press on with it?'

'I can't tie that gun to him. I'm working on that now.'

'It was found on his premises, wasn't it?'

'Under the seat in his car. But there were no fingerprints on
it. No prints on the rounds either.'

'But in *his* car. Locked wasn't it?'

'He says so.'

'In *his* garage?'

'Yes.'

'What more do you want? You've even got the actual flower worn at the time of the shooting – found in his dustbin – haven't you?'

'Yes.' Angel noticed the super's neck was a crimson hue.

'Mike, all I'm suggesting is that if the case is tight enough, then let's bring the CPS in now and save time. That's all. And let's get rid of these camp followers. Now what about it?'

Angel demurred. He shook his head. 'If you say so, John,' he said grudgingly.

The super sighed. 'Not if *I* say so. If *you* are ready.'

'Well I'm not ready, sir. I don't want to shove Jones into the dock until I'm certain he is guilty.'

'What?' roared Harker. 'You've gone soft on him.'

'No I haven't.'

'Well, I don't understand. I don't see any valid reason why you shouldn't pass the file over now. Right now! I'll tell you this, Mike. If it was any other Inspector, I would insist on it. I suppose you have some deep-down, secret underlying reason for not wanting to prosecute the man.'

'No, sir. It's not like that. I just haven't finished making a satisfactory case out yet. There are still some details.'

'Well get on with it!' bellowed the superintendent.

Angel didn't reply. He was thinking.

There was a short pause.

Harker impatiently held out his hands.

'Am I missing something, Mike? Is there something I don't know? What's holding everything up?'

'It's his reaction. He still refuses to take the indictment seriously. He won't have a solicitor. He doesn't put up any defence. He simply says he didn't do it and that's that.'

Harker was almost at screaming point.

'It's a textbook case: motive, opportunity and now means. All positive!'

Angel's hands tightened their grip on the chair arms. He breathed a long sigh.

'Mac supports the possibility – I put it no stronger than that – that Jones shot Charles Tabor, in a hypnotic trance or whatever without even knowing it.'

Superintendent Harker's mouth opened, then closed, then he said:

'What! I hope we are not going to have one of those stagey theatrical cases where expert witnesses waste the court's time with hypothetical notions and mumbo-jumbo!'

'It's not like that, John.'

'For god's sake keep away from hypnotists, psychiatrists and doctors! Murderers have been known to get off when so-called expert witnesses start spouting professional claptrap to the sort of juries we get round here!'

'It's not like that.'

'It had better not be. And don't keep saying: "It's not like that," because it bloody well is. I'll give you another forty-eight hours but that's the absolute limit. Do you understand?'

S E V E N

Angel went home that night highly dissatisfied. His work-load was stressful enough without the super adding to it with an ultimatum. He approached work the next day fully aware that the clock was ticking. He was in his office early and had disposed of some of the post, when Ahmed told him that Ingrid Dooley was here to see him.

'Thank you for coming to the station,' Angel said. 'Please sit down.'

Ingrid Dooley gave him her best Sunday smile, flashed the big eyelashes, unfastened the leather belt fastening her coat and elegantly lowered her trim, Chanel-sprayed body into the chair.

'I wanted to ask you a few questions,' Angel said.

She gave him a coy smile which made the dimple.

'Anything I can do to help.'

Angel screwed up his eyebrows. 'I have a feeling we met some time ago. I can't think where,' he said.

'I don't think so,' she replied with a broader smile.

'Your face seems so familiar.'

She brushed a piece of non-existent fluff off her black skirt, rattling the heavy gold bracelet on her wrist.

'People are always saying that to me.'

Angel rubbed the lobe of his ear. It must have sounded like

a chat-up line. But he was not in the chatting-up business. He looked at the slim white hands with the scarlet nails resting on her lap. The third finger of her left hand had no ring, but there was a two-carat blue-white diamond solitaire sitting conspicuously on the third finger of her other hand.

'Mmm.' Angel leaned back in his chair and briefly referred to his notebook. Then he looked up. 'At the time Charles Tabor was shot, where *were* you exactly? You weren't in your office?' he suggested.

'No, Inspector. Mr Tabor had asked me to take some orders and paperwork down to the dispatch department on the shop-floor.'

Angel raised his eyebrows. 'Oh? Wouldn't that have been a job for a junior?'

'Ordinarily yes, but there were some special instructions connected with the order. We had apparently sent a customer an item in error. It was only a small part. We were to send a replacement. This all needed explaining to the dispatch clerk; also it was important to get the part in the post that day. I had already prepared a letter for Mr Tabor promising that we would.'

Angel ran his tongue across his lips.

'Where were you when the shot was fired then?'

'I don't exactly know. I didn't hear it. I don't think anybody on the shop-floor heard it. I must have been on my way back to the office.'

'Is it noisy on the shop floor?'

'I hadn't thought so. I suppose it is.'

'What happened next?'

'I came up the stairs and into my office. At first I didn't realize anything was wrong until I heard some commotion from Mr Tabor's office. The door was open. I looked in and saw the girls from the general office gathered round his desk looking at the floor. One of them was screaming, the others were holding their heads in their hands. I rushed in and saw Mr Tabor on the floor. He had his hands across his stomach. Blood was oozing out between his fingers. It wasn't a pretty sight. I asked what had happened. The girl normally on reception, Rachel Honeycutt, was also there. She told me what she had seen and what the girls had told her. I came back to my own office, dialled 999 for an ambulance and then the police. Then I phoned Mark's office on the factory-floor. He wasn't there, so I told the girl to find him and ask him to come up urgently. That's about it.'

'And when did Mark Tabor arrive?'

'Oh, he came up a minute or two later, and then, after what seemed an endless time, the ambulance men arrived and then you were close on their heels.'

'Hmm. When I took over your office to do the questioning, you went out of the building, didn't you? Where did you go?'

'I just walked around the estate. It is a pleasant enough walk.'

Angel frowned. 'It was thawing, and raining. We had had a snowfall the night before. And it was quite windy.'

'I was well wrapped-up. I had a good pair of boots. I like walking. That office is so stuffy. We're on the fringe of the countryside. I had seen enough blood and mayhem for one day. I was glad to get outside. I had to think things out a bit.'

'What do you mean? What had you to think out?'

'My job for one thing. I had already thought I would have to look for something else, before Mr Tabor was murdered.'

'Mmm. You didn't actually see anything of the murder or the murderer then?'

'No.'

'Have you any idea why he would want to murder Charles Tabor?'

'It's no secret, Inspector. There was a long-standing dispute between Jones and Charles Tabor.'

'Go on, please.'

'Well, it started more than a year ago. Jones owed the firm two thousand pounds for office furniture and stuff supplied, and Mr Tabor was taking him to court for not paying for it. The hearing was next week. I don't know what will happen now.'

'And did he owe it?'

'Yes. Er – well, I assume he did. I knew the accounts office had been sending letters to him demanding payment, and I had written a letter for Mr Tabor to his solicitors instructing them to prosecute him.' She stopped, ran her tongue over her lips and, giving the policeman an old-fashioned look, said: 'I suppose if Charles Tabor thought he could get paid twice for something, he wouldn't hold back.'

'Oh?' Angel said, exaggerating a look of surprise. He looked at her closely.

After a few seconds she gave a little smile.

'Come on, Inspector. Don't let's pretend. I expect you know perfectly well that Charles Tabor was not exactly a hundred per cent straight.'

Angel shrugged slightly and leaned back in chair. He knew from experience he was about to be told a tale, and the teller was eager to tell it. All he had to do was sit back and listen.

'Why do you think I was looking round for another job?'

'I thought it was a good job. Comfortable working conditions. Your own office. Well paid,' he said craftily.

'Yes. It was well paid. It was all those things, but, from time to time, I had to do things I would rather not have done.'

'Like what?'

'Well, telling lies for him. Shutting a blind eye to some of the strokes he pulled.'

'For instance?'

'Well ...' she broke off. She looked down at the floor. 'I wish I hadn't started this.'

Angel smiled to himself. 'Go on.'

She hesitated, then said: 'Well, the safe was nearly always crammed full of cash.'

'Yes?'

'He used it for bribes to get orders ...' She stopped again. 'I am going to get myself into a lot of trouble telling you this.'

'Maybe you'd get into more trouble if you didn't.'

She didn't hesitate again. She dived straight in.

'Well, last September, he was anxious to get a big order from the government for computers and stuff – from the Department of Research and Development. Well, it was cash from that safe that was used to bribe the minister, a man called Eric Weltham, into giving him the order.'

'Mmm. Eric Weltham?'

Angel was surprised. His reaction didn't go unnoticed. The name seemed familiar, but he couldn't put it into any context.

'It was for millions!' she went on enthusiastically. 'That's why the factory is so busy.'

'How much was he paid?'

'A hundred thousand pounds. I overheard Mr Tabor telling Mark about it.'

'So it was quite common to have those sorts of sums in the safe, then?'

'Yes. Although I don't really know exactly how much was in there the day he was shot. It would be over a hundred thousand pounds. He never let anyone, including his own son Mark, near the keys.'

'Didn't he trust Mark, then?'

'I don't think he trusted anybody and they were always having rows about one thing or another.'

'About what?'

'About – er – anything, everything.'

'You must have overheard them.'

'They were always at it. Mark was always trying to do the right thing. And he was worried about this business with Eric Weltham. He felt it was very risky tapping an MP, especially a high profile cabinet minister like he is. I agreed with him but I never said so. It was nothing to do with me, besides, I had a job to protect and I wasn't ready to leave yet. I always came out of the office when I thought a row was brewing.'

'You're a very wise woman,' Angel said shrewdly.

She leaned back in the chair, raised her head, looked up at him and smiled, pleased that she had been able to impress him.

Angel knowingly smiled back. He deduced correctly that a bit of flattery would stand him in good stead with Ingrid Dooley.

'Do you happen to have the address of this MP chap, Eric Weltham?' he asked.

There was a knock at the door.

'Come in,' Angel called. It was Ahmed.

'I've done that job, sir,' he said, waving the videotape.

'Have you checked it, lad? Do you think it'll be all right?'

Ahmed looked at the inspector intently.

'It's what you said you wanted, sir.'

Angel took it from him and looked at the label.

'How long does it run?'

'About ninety seconds, sir. What you said. That's all.'

'Right,' said Angel. 'We'll have a look at it. Go down to the custody suite. Get the duty PC to let you take Jones to the CID office and when you are there, give me a buzz.'

Ahmed nodded. He went out and closed the door.

Angel put the tape down carefully on his desk. There was

anticipation in the air. He had a warm pounding in his chest. He had the feeling he was about make an important discovery about the Man in the Pink Suit. He rubbed his hands together like a rat catcher in a sewer.

The phone rang. He reached out for it.

'Angel.'

'Mac here.'

'Yes, Mac?'

'I've been looking up the side effects of diazepam, Mike. And there's one very interesting one.'

'Oh? What's that?'

'Impairment of memory.'

'Impairment of memory,' Angel said slowly. 'Impairment of memory. You mean he could have shot Tabor and now he can't remember it?'

'I do.'

'Hmmm?'

'Sounds a bit far-fetched, I know, but it happens. There's two recent cases in America. Ay. Also, I have another possible explanation.'

'Oh?'

'Ay. Had you considered that he might have been suffering from amnesia? That could have been brought on by a blow to the head, or through shock, or a massive change to the *status quo*.'

'Amnesia?'

'Ay. If he had fallen down stairs ... or had an accident in the car and hit his head ... or someone close to him, his nearest and dearest, had died unexpectedly ... or in a horrific way ... and perhaps he had witnessed it.'

'Any of these might have triggered amnesia?'

'Ay. Any one of them.' Then the doctor added pointedly, 'And subsequently, if he had absolutely no knowledge that he had murdered anyone, he would feel particularly incensed to be arrested for it, wouldn't he.'

Angel acknowledged that this was a fair point.

'And he'd be very convincing with his answers!' Mac went on. 'He wouldn't be acting. He'd be speaking from the heart. He'd be saying what he thought was true and smarting from what he saw as a totally unjust situation.'

Angel had to agree. He hadn't thought of amnesia at all.

'And he wouldn't remember *anything*?'

'He might not. Not a thing. That might be the explanation.'

'Thanks, Mac. Mmm.' Angel slowly replaced the phone, leaned back in the swivel-chair and closed his eyes. He rubbed his chin and sighed. What a turn-up for the book. Was it just possible that Jones had fallen down the cellar steps or something like that, or had had a great shock, or experienced some horrendous incident that had unbalanced him? Hmm. He thought about it for a while, then shook his head. He didn't like it. He didn't like it one bit. No. The elusive world of fantasy was knocking on the door. He could just visualize the witness-box swamped with so-called 'expert witnesses'. Psychiatrists, trying to look earnest, brought in by the defence and the prosecution, vying with each other to be believed by an artless jury. He didn't like the prospect one little bit. He could foresee the possibility of Jones getting away with blatant murder as a result of a smart city barrister in a Savile Row suit and a poncy haircut evoking all that guff about the accused being not guilty because the balance of his mind was disturbed.

Angel didn't want any of that. He had heard it all before. Some murderers had been freed on the strength of an accomplished barrister aided by a brilliant head doctor. Anyway, if he left things as they were, it wouldn't happen. The superintendent would hardly allow him to withdraw the case from the CPS unless there was some new, hard evidence. The magistrate's hearing would most certainly go ahead, the man in the pink suit would be remanded and the circus would undoubtedly move away from Bromersley nick.

Unless …

Angel was now ready to show Jones the CCTV. It was to be the man in the pink suit's last chance to come clean and admit he shot Charles Tabor.

The phone rang again. Right on cue. He opened his eyes and reached out.

'Angel?'

'We're ready for you, sir.'

'Right, Ahmed. Switch the machine on.'

He replaced the phone and sighed. The moment had arrived. He picked up the tape, went out of the office and down the green corridor. As he approached the CID Room, he could hear Jones's raised voice.

'I'm not an animal to be trundled here and there at anybody's whim. Where is the inspector?'

'I'm here,' Angel boomed as he came through the door.

The room was empty except for Jones and Ahmed.

Jones was standing with his hands on the back of a chair by the video-player. His face was red, his eyes were staring and his chest was heaving up and down. He stared at Angel with the look of a stripper whose G-string had just snapped.

Standing next to him was Ahmed with his mouth wide open.

Jones bristled angrily. 'What's happening? What's all this, Inspector?'

Angel took charge of the situation. He glared at the man. He realized for the first time how ill-tempered it was possible for him to be.

'Sit down,' he boomed authoritatively. Then he turned to Ahmed. 'Close your mouth, lad. I don't want to see what you had for your dinner.' He pointed to the chairs. 'Both of you, sit down.'

'I really must protest at being pushed about from pillar to post like this,' said Jones, still red in the face.

Jones and Ahmed both sat down.

Angel put up a protesting hand.

'Mr Jones, you are about to see a video of yourself. It's important. Look at the screen.'

Jones's jaw dropped. His eyes lost their intensity and he blinked. He gave a short sigh and relaxed his shoulders. He smiled slightly.

'Oh? Is it something I've recorded recently?'

'Oh yes,' Angel said meaningfully. 'Oh yes. Very recently.' He pushed the tape firmly into the slot. 'Now watch this carefully.'

Angel stood at forty-five degrees to the video screen so that he could observe Jones's reactions.

The screen was about four feet by three feet, and the picture, which was slightly fuzzy, was in black-and-white. The picture briefly showed the reception area at the factory. A man in a light suit appeared with his back to the camera.

Jones sat upright and stared at the screen. He turned briefly to Angel.

'Whereabouts is this?' he asked urgently.

Angel didn't reply.

The film showed the man run up the stairs into Tabor's office, stand in front of the desk, pull the gun out of his pocket and fire it. Tabor fell across his desk and on to the floor.

Jones eyes opened wider as he stared at the screen, his jaw dropped.

'When was this? Where was this?'

The picture on the screen then showed the man rush swiftly down the stairs and out of the picture. The screen went blank. The tape had ended.

Jones turned to face Angel.

'I demand to know where that was filmed and who the photographer was.'

Angel turned to Ahmed.

'We'll go in the interview room, lad. Take charge of that tape and follow us in there.'

He nodded.

Jones stood up. He faced Angel square on. Suddenly he seemed to have a lot to say. He spoke quickly.

'It was not me, you know. It's nothing like me. That man's fatter than me. I don't walk like that either. I'm not a pansy. I may not be married but I'm not a poof. I may get married one day, if I meet the right woman. That man is quite obviously a homosexual. He swings his hips from one side to the other, like a woman. Homosexuals walk like that. He's nothing like me. Who is it impersonating me? That's what I'd like to know.'

Angel shook his head.

'Come on, sir. Let's go in the interview room. We can talk there,' he added as he moved into the corridor.

Jones followed.

'It's not me, you know,' he continued with a finger moving excitedly as he walked. Then he pointed back at the video screen. 'I don't look like that. It's ridiculous. It's a put up job. That's *not* me, I tell you.'

Ahmed came from behind them to the interview room door. He opened it and the three of them went in.

'It's a caricature of me. It's not for real. It's not me. It's an actor fellow. An impersonator. Must be ... somebody trying to cash in on my celebrity status.'

The heat of the room hit them. It was very warm and stuffy

and a sickly smell of polish or similar met them as they entered the room. Jones's nose began to twitch. He sniffed several times, and searched for a handkerchief. He found one and held it to his nose, then continued:

'And that suit is a disgrace. It is rubbish, nothing like the quality of my suit. It's a pity your pictures aren't in colour. You would see that the colour is different. My suit is an entirely different shade. It's darker. And it is better cut. Look at the lapels for a start, and the waist. It's not a patch on the suit I wear. That suit of mine cost me a thousand pounds.'

Angel pointed to a chair at one side of the table.

'Sit there.' He looked round the room. The stuffy smell annoyed him. He looked up to the windows and found they were both fastened. He opened them both and set the catches on maximum. The smell of clear air was pleasing.

Jones dropped pensively into the seat, wiping his eyes with a handkerchief.

Angel turned to Ahmed and nodded towards the door.

'Fetch three teas, lad.'

The cadet nodded.

'And leave the door open. Let's get some air in here. Phew.'

Ahmed nodded.

Jones sat tentatively on the edge of the chair. He began strange movements with his hands on the tabletop as if he was kneading invisible dough.

'It's not me. That tape is faked. It's surprising what they can do with technology these days. They can make quasi-humans from computer images. It's amazing what can be done.'

Angel leaned over to the recording-machine and switched it on. The red light glowed. He checked the tape was running, then he said:

'Interview with Frank Percival Jones, Thursday, twentieth January, fourteen-forty hours. Present, DI Angel.'

Angel looked across the table at Jones. The strange movements with the hands continued. His watery eyes stared
unfocused across the room at the wall. Angel noticed this and
it worried him. He had not seen this sort of behaviour before.
The man's face had lost its healthy-looking ruby hue and his
hair looked lighter or greyer and a few strands lay across an
eye. The policeman looked closely at him again. Was he ill?
Was he going to play the nut-case card?

'Are you all right, sir?'

The man was deep in thought. He lifted his head. The
corners of his mouth were turned down. The kneading business stopped. He stared at Angel for a few seconds.

'What?' he said.

'Are you all right?'

Jones didn't reply. He looked down at his hands again.

Ahmed came in with a tin tray holding three plastic cups of
tea. Angel took two cups from the tray and put one of them
on the table in front of him.

'Here. Tea.'

Jones looked at him with a vacant expression.

Angel took a sip from the other cup and then smacked his
lips.

'That's better.' He turned to the recording-machine. 'For
the benefit of the tape, Cadet Ahaz has just joined us.' Then
he pointed to the chair next to him. 'Sit down, lad.'

He looked across the table at the man.

'Drink up, sir. You'll feel better.'

Jones looked up, blinked and reached out a hand. He put
the cup to his lips. His eyes were half-closed. His complexion
was returning to normal. He put the cup down.

Angel rubbed his chin.

'Well, now then, sir. Let's stop playing bloody silly games,
shall we?'

'I do not play games, Inspector,' Jones replied, his voice rising an octave.

Angel pulled the small key and key-ring out of his pocket and dangled it in front of Jones.

'Is this yours?'

Jones mouth opened and a smile briefly appeared.

'Oh. Where did you get that?' He reached out to take it from him.

Angel pulled away.

'What is it for? What does it open?'

Jones's expression changed instantly to a scowl.

'It has nothing to do with you. It's mine, and I'll have it, thank you.'

Angel put it back in his pocket.

'What does it open?'

'Mind your own business. Where did you find it?'

'Is it something that is secret? Is it something you don't want me to know about?'

'Well, yes. No. It has nothing to do with you.'

'Is it the key to the hiding-place of the money?'

'No. What money?'

'The hundred thousand pounds.'

'I don't know what you are talking about.'

'Come on, Frank. The hundred thousand pounds that was in Charles Tabor's safe.'

'Certainly not. I don't know anything about that. Like everything else, Inspector, you are barking up the wrong tree. I want to tell you … I want to tell you, categorically, that it was positively *not* me on that tape. It was obviously an impostor posing as me. I don't care if he *was* wearing a pink suit. It doesn't prove a thing.'

Angel was unmoved. He shook his head.

'And how many men do you think there are walking around

in pink suits, for goodness sake?'

'You see. You don't believe anything I say.'

'I'm trying to. Believe me. Well, let's have the truth from now on, shall we?'

'I have always told you the truth,' said Jones with a tremor in his voice.

Angel tightened his lips. He was going to pursue the argument but decided against it.

'Did you notice what shoes the man on the tape was wearing?'

'No.'

'He was wearing suede shoes. They appeared to be brown suede shoes. There were enough shots to be certain they were suede shoes. When you are dressed up in your pink suit for the television, what sort of shoes do you wear?'

'Brown suede shoes,' said Jones after a long pause.

The policeman nodded slowly.

'And did you notice the gold ring on his right hand?'

'No.'

'It's exactly like the one you are wearing now. Exactly.'

'One plain wedding ring is very much like another.'

'Did you notice the rest of the outfit?'

'Yes.'

'It's precisely the same as you wear in every particular, isn't it. Even down to the buttonhole.'

'Yes. But it can all be duplicated, easily. It doesn't prove a thing. And the suit was tatty. I don't suppose you noticed that. You could see how badly it was cut. And it needed pressing. The sunglasses and the hat would disguise his face.'

Angel rubbed his chin. 'You're not impressing me any, you know.' He sighed. 'I wonder if you'll have any better luck with a jury?' He shook his head. 'Somehow I doubt it.'

'It's obvious it's not me,' snapped Jones. 'A blind man on a galloping horse could see that. Look at the way he walked. He was obviously a poof!'

Angel shook his head.

'That man looked like you, because it was you. Four people who saw you in the flesh are all prepared to swear on oath it was you. And they were not looking at videotape. They haven't even seen this tape. They were looking at you.'

Jones eyes lit up. His face reddened.

'How many times do I have to tell you?' he yelled.' He banged a fist on the table. '*It wasn't me!*' he screamed.

'Very well,' Angel said drily.

He was diffident at putting the next question. He didn't want to show the man a possible easy way out. However, in the interests of justice, it was necessary for the question to be put.

'Have you ever been hypnotized?' he asked quietly.

'Hypnotized?' echoed Jones, his eyes flashing. 'No.'

Angel thought the answer came too quickly.

'Are you certain?'

'Positive.'

'I don't mean necessarily in a theatre or a studio or a night-club environment, as an entertainment.'

'No.'

'Not for medical, psychological reasons?'

Jones's eyes lit up again.

'Certainly not. *No!*'

He seemed positive about that, Angel mused. There was still the possibility he had been hypnotized without realizing it. Or was he simply lying? Angel could do nothing about that. He moved on.

'Have you had any sort of an accident lately?'

The man looked weary.

'What sort of an accident?'

'Any sort. In the car. At home. Falling down stairs. In the bath. Hitting your head on a shelf. I don't know. You'll have a cellar in your house, I suppose. Have you fallen down the steps? Anything?'

'What a strange question. No. I have not,' retorted Jones angrily.

'Just checking. Just checking. Eliminating a few things.'

'Come along, Inspector, if you are not releasing me then lead me back to my cell. Stupid questions! At least I can get a bit of peace and quiet there. This room smells awful. And I want those tranquillizers you took from me. I have every right to them. They were properly prescribed for me by a doctor. They are mine. I want them back.'

Angel sniffed. He had no intention of giving him the diazepam.

'We'll have to see about those, sir. You'll not be appearing in front of your public for a bit yet.'

Jones began drumming his fingers on the table.

'I want to go back to my room. I don't like it in here. Let me out of here. This treatment is insufferable!'

Angel was determined to continue.

'I have nearly finished the questions, sir. Tell me, how is your family?'

'What family? I have no family.'

'Father, mother, brothers and sisters?'

'My father and mother are long gone. I was an only child. I have some cousins somewhere. Canada, I believe. I have not seen them for years and I have no wish to.'

'Friends?'

'No. I have no friends. My agent is the nearest I have to a friend, and there are times when he is a nuisance. He can be very boring.'

'Anybody in your circle died recently?'

'I haven't got a circle,' Jones said quickly and then suddenly his eyes lit up, and waving his hand in the air added, 'Ha! You're going to suggest I cut their throats with a palette-knife, aren't you?'

Angel rubbed his chin slowly. He looked at the man. Jones's face was bright red. His collar was curled up on one side. The burgundy bow-tie was askew. A few more strands of fair hair flopped across an eye. His lips, usually tight, controlled and still, now twitched and moved involuntarily. Purple patches showed through the pink of his lips. His long fingers tapped indecipherable Morse code nervously on the tabletop. This was a very different man from the one Angel had first interviewed among his antique furniture in his house two days ago.

'No, sir,' Angel said quietly. 'Believe it or not, I am trying to be helpful. I am trying to find a reason why you behave the way you do.'

Jones gave a long sigh.

'I behave the way I do because I am being asked such stupid and irrelevant questions. No. Nobody close to me has died recently.'

Angel nodded. 'When was the last time you saw a doctor?'

'Years and years ago. I enjoy excellent health.'

'Well, when did your doctor prescribe the diazepam, then?'

'Oh?' Jones looked down and then up, and said, 'I bought them in a shop. A chemist's shop.'

'You can't *buy* them. They're on prescription only.'

'Ah yes, I remember. I bought them when I was in Antwerp recently. Making a programme on Frans Hals. They haven't got such silly restrictive laws over there.'

'The label is written in English. They must have been supplied by a chemist in Britain.'

'No.' Jones shrugged. 'Well, I don't remember.'

'You must have had a prescription from a doctor in the UK.'

Jones put a hand to his temple. He shook his head. 'Well, I can't remember.'

'Ever had amnesia?'

'Amnesia? No! Certainly not.'

'Are you sure? You can't remember how you came by these pills?'

'I will remember, and when I do, I will tell you,' Jones said, rocking his head angrily from side to side. 'I have an excellent memory. I never forget a face or a name. I can rattle off names, dates and titles of every dominant artist in the world,' he said, waving an expressive hand in the air.

Angel had only one more question for him that afternoon. But it was a vital one, and he didn't expect to get a satisfactory answer. He delivered it quickly.

'Where did you get the gun from?'

Jones's jaw dropped. He hesitated.

'What gun?'

'The gun hidden in your car. The Walther. The one that killed Charles Tabor.'

Jones threw up both hands. His eyes flashed.

'There *is* no gun in my car. I don't *have* a gun. I don't *own* a gun. I wouldn't know how to *fire* a gun if I had one.' He got to his feet. He dabbed his watering eyes. 'This is intolerable. How many times do I have to tell you I didn't shoot that man. It must have been somebody dressed like me. If you found a gun in my car, you must have planted it there. If you didn't, well one of your stooges must have put it there. I certainly don't know the first thing about it.'

'It just appeared there from nowhere?' Angel said drily. 'Was your car locked?'

'Of course it was locked. I always lock my car.' Jones took

out a white silk handkerchief from his top pocket, wiped his forehead and resumed his seat. 'I suppose I have to take your word for it that there is a gun.'

'It was found in your locked car, under the seat.'

'Ridiculous! It must have been put there. I understand that no special talent is required these days to break into a car.'

'They'd have to break into your garage first.'

Jones jumped up again. He folded his arms in a defiant gesture.

'I am not saying another word until I have spoken to a solic- itor.'

'Ah!' Angel smiled. He was glad that Jones was seeing sense and taking the crime seriously. 'It's about time, Mr Jones. It's only since I told you we had found the gun that you realize how serious the situation is.'

Jones' eyes closed momentarily. He leaned over the table and put his shaking hands palms down on the top. His lips were thin, tight and blue. His eyes narrowed as he stared at Angel. He spoke quietly but as gravely as a judge in a black cap.

'I know what your game is, Inspector. You are trying to prove that I am ill, and that I murdered that man while in a trance or illness of some kind. Well, I didn't. I have full control over my mind and my memory at all times. I am an educated man, an academic. I am not some ill-educated, drugged-up youth who will crack under your questioning and confess to anything you care to suggest to him. You are in for a fight. You would like me to crack under your interrogation. Well, I won't. You cannot brainwash me into thinking I murdered a man simply because you have pictures of someone in a pink suit similar to mine waving a gun around—'

Angel's patience was up.

'Not *a* gun. Not *any* old gun. *The* gun. The actual gun that killed Charles Tabor. Only *that* gun was used. Ballistics prove it. It couldn't have been any other. That is a fact. And it was found deliberately concealed in your locked car!'

Suddenly, Jones's head dropped. He crumpled down into the seat, his head hit the table, his arms splayed out in front. He was motionless.

Angel stood up and leaned over him. He turned the man's head to one side and put two fingers on his neck searching for a pulse.

Ahmed stood up, his jaw dropped. He looked anxiously at Jones and then at the Inspector.

Angel turned to him.

'Well don't just stand there, lad. Get a doctor!'

EIGHT

The doo-dah wail of the ambulance siren brought Superintendent Harker in shirt sleeves charging out of his office and racing up the green corridor. Angel, hands in pockets, head down was making his way from the back door of the station to his office. He had just seen an unconscious Frank P Jones on a stretcher, an oxygen mask across his face and a drip sachet being held by a paramedic, being speedily loaded into an ambulance. It was surrounded by a fevered, chattering crowd of television cameramen, photographers and reporters surging round the stretcher and the ambulance doors, as the medics made an urgent bid to get the man away to Bromersley General. Angel had quickly conscripted PC Scrivens, from the reception counter, to accompany and guard the prisoner.

The superintendent and the inspector met abruptly outside Angel's office door.

'What the hell's going on?' roared Harker.

Angel shrugged. 'It's Jones. He fainted or something. I sent for a doctor.'

'What did you do to him?'

Angel's jaw stiffened. 'Nothing!' he replied angrily.

'Is that siren one of ours?'

'It's an ambulance. They've carted him off to the hospital.'

'Is he going to be all right?'

'Don't know.'

Harker pulled a face. 'Can't do with a death while in custody job. He's alive, I hope?'

'Yes. I think so.'

'How bad is he?'

'Bad. An attack of asthma or something.'

'Come into my office.'

The superintendent led the way. They walked down the corridor in silence. The door was open. Once inside, Harker closed the door and pointed to a chair.

Angel sat down.

'What happened?'

'A normal interview. A normal *final* interview. I was closing down all the alternative options of his story and facing him with the inevitable facts, that's all.'

'Hmmm.' Harker grunted, scowled and shook his head.

'He got very wound up.'

Harker's eyes flashed. 'Ah.'

Angel sensed disapproval. He headed it off.

'Cadet Ahaz was there. It was being taped. It was all very proper.'

'Hmm. Glad you've got a record,' said Harker, relieved. 'Oh.' His shoulders dropped. He sighed, then nodded. 'Good. Good.'

There was a slight pause. Angel made to stand up.

'If there's nothing else, John?'

'Ay. Hang on a minute,' he said, waving him to sit down. 'You know, we should have got him to court, Mike. Then this would never have happened here. All this would have happened in Armley nick.'

Angel didn't reply.

'Is he going to die?' Harker asked brusquely.

Angel shrugged. 'Hope not.'

'Are you ready to push this to court now?'

'My forty-eight hours aren't up till tomorrow morning, sir.'

'No. But, well, he's in hospital ...'

'Come on, John. Let's see what happens between now and then, eh?'

Harker nodded. 'What are you doing about this MP chap, Eric Weltham? Are you going to be able to make out a case?'

'No.'

Harker growled and pulled an angry face. 'I don't like it.'

'I've hardly had time to think about it,' said Angel. 'I can't just let him get away with it, can I?'

'On that girl's evidence alone, you'll have to!'

Angel nodded. It was true.

Angel drove his car purposefully along Sheffield Road. A line of traffic ahead caused him to apply the brakes. He rolled to a stop behind a beer wagon. He peered forward. He couldn't see the beginning of the queue or the cause of the delay. He knew a short cut down St John's Road that would bring him into the Mawdsley Estate, on to Damon Street, along Park Street, then Clarendon Street and up to a T-junction, then he could turn right on to Charles Street and up to the top to rejoin Sheffield Road. He edged forward and turned left off the main road on to St John's Road. He made a few twists and turns up to the T-junction, where he had to slow down behind a car. The driver ahead was nervously about to make the turning. It was providential that he was delayed. Angel looked left and then right in preparation to making the turn.

That was when he saw him! It was Spotty Minto. A pasty-faced scruff leaning on a wall with his hands in his pockets outside Charles Street post office smoking a cigarette and conspicuously failing to look inconspicuous. Spotty had a foot up backwards against the wall by the door of the double-fronted terraced shop. He was in his thirties, wearing a woolly hat, leather jacket and jeans. He wasn't called Spotty for nothing. His face had more holes in it than a pub dartboard.

Angel quickly pulled the steering-wheel hard over to the left, and stopped with two wheels on the pavement. Three other cars were parked outside the two little shops at each the side of the post office. There were no signs of anybody else in the street.

Spotty looked across and saw Angel getting out of the car. He spat out the lighted cigarette on to the pavement and made off hastily in the opposite direction with his hands in his pockets.

Angel immediately called: 'Hey, Spotty!'

A woman with a shopping-bag came out of the butcher's shop. She looked at the policeman. Her mouth opened then closed. She made a beeline for the newsagents next door.

Spotty Minto kept walking away, his head down, looking at the flagstones, his hands in his pockets, and increasing his speed.

Angel stood his ground outside the front of the post office door.

'If you don't come back here, Spotty, I'll put a warrant out for your arrest,' he bellowed.

The man took four more steps, stopped, hovered and turned round. He raised his head slightly and glanced up. His mouth dropped open and, with his head still down he ambled slowly back until he was twenty feet from the policeman.

'Didn't know it was you, Inspector. Honest, I didn't,' he called. He had a high-pitched voice and spoke like a school-girl trying to convince her father, the bishop, that the swelling would be a virgin birth. 'Otherwise I would have come the first time. I haven't done anything wrong you know. I was just waiting. That's all. I mean there's no law against waiting, now is there?'

Angel pointed downwards with a finger to a spot three feet in front him.

'Come here, lad.'

Spotty Minto's thick-soled shoes brought him silently into position. His shifty eyes kept sliding towards the post-office door and back.

'What are you doing, lad?'

Spotty sniffed. 'Waiting.'

Angel began to walk round him. 'What for?'

Spotty shrugged.

The policeman noticed the bulging back pocket of the jeans.

'What have you got in there, Spotty?'

'Where?'

Angel dug into it and pulled out a wad of notes fastened by an elastic band.

'Here, what you doing?' protested Spotty.

'Playing at Robin Hood?'

'Eh? That's *my* money.'

The post-office door opened. An old lady with a face as wrinkled as a pound of tripe came out. She was holding her pension book and some money in her hand. She looked uneasy at seeing Angel and Spotty looking at her. Spotty Minto turned away. He stared at the pavement and covered one side of his face with a hand. It would be a disaster to meet this woman in front of the policeman. He desperately wanted to disappear. He wished Endora would arrive and cast a spell.

The old lady looked from one to the other and then back to the Inspector.

'Excuse me,' she said forlornly, holding out some money. 'I have to see this young man.'

Angel smiled sweetly at her.

'It's all right, dear. He doesn't want it. I'm his boss. The slate is wiped clean. You don't owe us anything.' He pushed the money he had taken from the man's back pocket into her hand. 'Here's some of last week's back. It was too much. But take some advice. Don't borrow money from Mr McCallister again. All right?'

Her eyes lit up. 'Ooooh. Thanks, young man. No, I won't. Oh no, I *won't*.'

She toddled off, counting the wad of notes Angel had given her.

Angel turned back to the man. The smile had gone. He grabbed him by the collar. And with his finger an inch from his nose, he wagged it and said:

'You leave that old biddy alone, do you hear? Unless you want to go down again for a four-year-stretch.'

'Oh no, Mr Angel. Oh no,' squealed Spotty Minto.

'I won't warn you again. Next time, I won't be so soft with you. Do you understand?'

'Yes. *Yes!*'

'And you can tell Tiny McCallister what I've told you,' said Angel, pushing Spotty against the wall and releasing hold of the collar. Then he sniffed. He turned up his nose as if he'd just opened a sewer. 'And for God's sake, get a bath, and a proper job, and keep out of trouble.'

He turned away angrily, and made for his car, trying to rub away invisible muck from between his thumb and finger as he went. He was soon back on the main Sheffield Road and on his way to Eric Weltham's house, two miles out of the centre of Bromersley. He checked the address Ingrid Dooley had so readily provided. He was looking for 455 Sheffield Road. He followed the numbers up to it. There was a smart block of twenty-four newly built flats with gardens, and a tarmac drive in the process of being completed out at the front. He noticed posters in the windows that read: Luxury Flats To Let, long or short lease: Apply Telephone Bromersley 394297. The high block was at the opposite side of the road and was a good landmark for locating Eric Weltham's modern, large, red-brick and detached mansion. It looked expensive and well-maintained. The front lawn looked as if it had just been returned from Sketchley's. The house stood high on a ridge in line with other similar houses whose large private rear-gardens faced south with a view across fields towards the M1 motorway. The drone of traffic could almost always be heard from the garden without being able to see a single vehicle. The drive gates were open and on the Italian-tiled drive in front of a double garage was parked a big American car. Someone was home. Angel nodded approvingly as he stopped by the kerb and pulled on the handbrake.

He went up the short front path and pressed the bell. He then fished in his coat pocket for his ivory card-case and took out a card in readiness.

The door was opened promptly by a smart, young man in a cream lightweight summer suit. He had bleached blond hair, white shirt, tie and white deck-shoes. He held on to the door handle and looked Angel up and down, taking in every detail.

'Yes?'

The policeman switched on his Sunday smile, leaned forward and offered the card.

'I am Inspector Angel from Bromersley Police,' he said. 'I want to see Mr Eric Weltham.'

The young man took the card but didn't look at it.

'Have you any means of identification?' he said in a cockney voice.

Angel looked up into the steely blue eyes of the man. He had not called on a cabinet minister before. Was this the new style of security men the Home Office provided?

THE MAN IN THE PINK SUIT

Angel put his hand up to his inside pocket.

The young man stiffened.

Angel noticed.

'Just getting my warrant card out, lad,' he said quietly. 'There's nothing to get excited about.'

He slowly pulled out his wallet using the tips of his extended first and second fingers, opened it and showed it to the man.

The man looked at it for a few seconds.

'Are you satisfied, lad?' Angel asked.

'That'll do me.'

The door was then suddenly pulled open further and a chubby young woman in a big loose fitting housecoat with a lot of long blond hair falling around her head in all directions came round the edge of it. She had obviously been monitoring this introduction from behind the door.

'Of course you can see Eric. Please come in. He's on the phone at the moment.' She reached out, took the card, glanced at it, passed it back to the young man and pointed upstairs. 'Nigel will tell him you're here.'

The young man turned away and left the hallway. The woman closed the front door. Angel heard the latch click.

'Come this way, Inspector.'

Angel looked at her. He felt he knew her from somewhere.

'Excuse my appearance,' she said loudly as she flounced down the hall. 'I've just got out of the bath. We're getting ready to fly to Nice for a concert and dinner. Isn't it a hoot?' she said with an excited giggle.

She saw him staring.

'Oh. I'm not married to Mr Weltham,' she said chirpily, forcing a smile. 'Eric is in the throes of divorcing her. Please come in here.'

It was a very comfortable looking sitting-room, furnished with two three-piece suites, two fireside chairs, a coffee-table, a small bar and a large teak cabinet which Angel supposed housed a television set, video and whatever else. Everything was light in colour, spotless and uncluttered.

'Please sit down, Inspector. I'm Louella Panter.'

'Oh yes,' Angel said. 'I thought I knew you from somewhere.'

She flashed an attractive smile. 'Television people are soon forgotten. My show has been off the air for two weeks and nobody knows me.' She giggled.

Angel recalled she was the woman who hosted the new popular television panel quiz game: *What's in it for me?* He had seen it once on a Saturday evening. He didn't think much to it, but it seemed to be popular. The winner was the player who was insulted the most and embarrassed the least for money for half an hour. Knowledge and intelligence were not in great demand from the players or the audience. It wasn't Angel's choice in entertainment.

'Would you like a drink?'

'No, thank you.'

Angel thought it was difficult to believe she was the glamorous woman he had seen on the screen. She looked shorter, chubbier, had wrinkles above her nose and her face was a patchwork of red blotches.

The young man with the bleached hair came into the room.

'He's coming, Lou.'

'This is Nigel Coldwell, Inspector,' said Louella Panter. 'I don't know where I'd be without him. He looks after me. And Eric, of course.'

The young man gave her a blank look.

Angel noticed it. Louella didn't.

The inspector nodded at Nigel Coldwell.

'Hi,' the man said with hardly a glance. He looked towards Louella.

'The Inspector doesn't want a drink, Nigel,' she said.

Coldwell went out of the room.

'You won't keep Eric long, will you?' said Louella. 'We have to leave for the airport soon.'

There were mutterings in the hall. It was Weltham exchanging words with Nigel. Then he came in. He was in a smart pin-striped suit, crisp collar and tie. He waved a small cigar at the policeman and smiled.

Angel recognized him straight away. He looked and spoke exactly as he did on television. It was surprising that Louella appeared so different. He made to get up out of the chair. Weltham waved him down.

'Now, Inspector, you are from the local force?'

'Yes sir.' Angel nodded.

The MP flopped into an easy-chair next to him.

Louella was leaning across the back of the settee, holding a glass in her hand.

Weltham glared meaningfully at her.

She waved the glass at him and said pertly: 'It's only tonic, Eric. It's only tonic.' She looked at Angel. 'He doesn't want me to drink, Inspector. I have to get trim before I start recording my new series in two weeks.'

Weltham turned to the Inspector.

'What did you want to see me about?'

'Can we speak privately, sir?'

Louella's eyebrows shot up.

'Oh. Not to worry,' she said. 'You boys stay here. I'll go and get dressed. You won't be long, darling, will you?' She sailed off through the glass door and closed it behind her.

Eric Weltham pulled the cigar out of his mouth and leaned towards Angel.

'Is it a security matter?' he asked quietly.

'No sir. No. But I'll come straight to the point. You may

have heard that Charles Tabor, the man with the big computer factory on the Northrop estate was murdered in his office on Monday morning last.'

'Oh yes. That odd fellow in the pink suit shot him, didn't he? The arty crafty chap on television.'

Angel nodded. 'Well, there's a matter of a hundred thousand pounds missing from the safe in Charles Tabor's office.'

Eric Weltham's jaw stiffened momentarily. 'Really? That was the motive, then?'

'We are not sure about that, sir. It wasn't taken at the time of the murder.'

'Well – erm – what's this got to do with me?'

Angel said nothing. He looked into Weltham's eyes.

The MP looked straight back at him. Then he broke away to stub the cigar butt in an ashtray on the chair-arm. His lips moved as if he was about to say something but he remained silent.

Angel leaned across to him. 'A little bird told me that you knew something about it, sir,' he said, in a very small voice.

Weltham's eyes narrowed. 'I don't know what you are talking about, man,' he replied quietly and evenly.

'You knew Charles Tabor. You've met him.'

'What if I have?'

'You approved a big order for your Department, the Department for Research and Development, for computer hardware and I understand that in response to that, in September last, you were paid a hundred thousand pounds in cash.'

Eric Weltham got to his feet. His face was red.

'This conversation terminates right here, Inspector Angel. I am an MP and a Privy Counsellor.'

Angel rose. He was undeterred.

'I know that, sir. I know that only too well.'

'Who is suggesting that I knew anything about stolen money?' frothed Weltham. 'I'll sue them for every penny they've got. Who is it?'

There was a gentle tap on the door. Louella Panter appeared. Her hair was now in some sort of order. The wrinkles above her nose were no longer visible and the red blotches on her face were hidden under a layer of make-up. She was wearing a short, floral-patterned dress too tight at the bust and furrowed across the hips. Angel thought the dress more appropriate for someone younger.

'Excuse me, chaps,' she chirped. Then she looked at Angel. 'Is the inspector staying for a quick cup of tea?'

'The inspector's leaving,' Weltham said heavily.

'Oh. Right, Eric.' She went out, pulled the door to and then immediately reopened it. 'I'm ready when you are.'

'Right, Lou.'

She closed the door.

'You won't assist me with my enquiries then, sir?'

'No. Not I won't, I can't. I know nothing about any money, stolen or otherwise. The Civil Service made the final decision as to which tender to accept, and I understand Tabor's was the best on the day,' replied Weltham sternly.

'I will inform the chief constable accordingly,' Angel said drily.

Weltham sniffed. 'You do whatever you have to do, Inspector. You haven't told me who's been suggesting that I know anything about stolen money.'

Angel tapped the side of his nose with a forefinger.

'Information received, sir. I can't say more than that.'

Eric Weltham pulled an angry face. The interview was over. He turned towards the door.

A doorbell rang. Two pairs of feet sped along the hall.

Weltham went to the room door, opened it and listened

into the hall. Angel stood behind him.

The front door was opened. Angel heard Nigel's cockney voice.

'Oh. Good afternoon, Mrs Tassell.'

A woman's small voice said, 'I've brought these for Miss Panter.'

'Oh, very well,' Louella said brusquely. 'Take them, Nigel, quickly. We're just going out, Mrs Tassell. I must go. I'll phone you.'

'Yes of course, Miss Panter.'

The door closed quickly.

Nigel rushed past carrying a large brown-paper bag held in his arms in front of him and made for the stairs. Louella followed.

Weltham opened the room door and led Angel into the hall.

Louella Panter turned on the stairs.

'Are you leaving, Inspector? Sorry we have to dash. Nice to have met you.'

'Thank you. Goodbye.'

Weltham opened the front door.

'Goodbye, sir.'

'Goodbye.'

The front door closed with a bang.

Angel dashed down the path to the pavement and looked along the road in each direction eager not to lose the visitor, a Mrs Tassell. He spotted a small car travelling towards Bromersley, its outline diminishing with every second until it disappeared completely as the road curved away. He bounced into his car, made speed along the road and eventually caught up with it. He noted the index number, then surged forward to overtake it. He observed that the driver was a small grey-haired lady, hunched over the steering wheel and gripping it as if it was trying to get away from her. He would make contact with her in due course.

He pressed harder on the accelerator to the next junction. He drove down a crescent and made a right turn to bring him back on to Sheffield Road facing the opposite direction and travelled along until he reached the new block of flats opposite Weltham's house. He slowed down and noted with satisfaction that the big American car had gone. He stopped the car, lowered the window and looked up to the house eaves, the garage, the outbuildings, then across to the telegraph-poles and trees. He was looking for CCTV cameras. He could see no signs of any.

He got out of the car, went up the path and rang the front doorbell again. This time, he didn't want to find anybody in. He was not disappointed. He waited a minute or two and then casually looked around. He took in all the windows of the neighbours and satisfied himself that he was not being observed. He sauntered round the side of the house on a concrete path past the side door to the garden. He looked down the crazy-paving path across a big lawn to the end of the area that looked out to fields. He could hear a flock of bored sheep bleating and munching in the field and the sound of motorway traffic beyond.

He didn't know what he was doing there, or what he was trying to find. He certainly didn't expect to find £100,000 sticking out from under a grass sod. He took in the two big greenhouses and noticed some early tomato and spring plants through closed, steamed up windows. Next to them was a garden shed. He tried the door. It was locked. He glanced down at the purpose built sun-trap at the side and the rose arbour beyond the lawn. He came back towards the house, passing a large glass-and-metal sun-lounge built as a lean-to against the room he guessed would be the dining room.

Round the corner, he saw a brick-built area where dustbins were kept. It housed two galvanized metal bins. It was spotless. He raised the bin lids. They were both lined with clean plastic bags and held no rubbish.

Angel pulled a face. It was annoying. Dustbins were a detective's stock in trade. He lifted them up. On the concrete floor under one of the bins was part of a small plastic capsule: the sort that might have held pills. It was about the diameter of a test tube and about three inches long. Only part of the container was there. The top was splintered and had jagged points towards where the cap or stopper might have been. It looked as if it might have dropped out of an overfull bin carelessly handled, and then been damaged by having the rim on the base of the bin slammed down on top of it. He looked on the floor of the area to see if there were any fractured pieces but it had been recently swept. He held the part-capsule up to the light. He could see a few grains of a red powder sticking to the inside bottom of it. It wasn't dried blood. It wasn't a drug familiar to him. He had no idea what the substance was, but he knew Mac would tell him. And he also knew instinctively that that *ménage à trois* needed looking at more closely.

NINE

The following morning, Angel bought a copy of the *Northern Daily Echo* on his way into the office. The headline was stunning and magnetic. He settled in his chair to read it:

MAN IN PINK SUIT NEAR DEATH!

Frank P Jones, the man in the pink suit, collapsed and was raced to hospital by ambulance in a mercy dash. He fainted during interrogation by a senior police officer in Bromersley police station at 3 pm yesterday afternoon.

This dramatic turn of events began when Jones was arrested yesterday and charged with the murder of local industrialist, Charles Tabor in his office in front of four witnesses.

Jones denies the charge.

The well-known art critic and TV star was admitted to a private ward in Bromersley General Hospital under armed guard.

Buxom beauty, Louella Panter, celebrity panel-game hostess, who also lives in the town, when asked about Jones is reported as saying: 'I've never heard of the stupid man.'

Full report inside. See pages 4 – 11.

There was a knock at the door.

'Come in,' Angel grunted.

It was Ahmed. Angel looked up from the paper.

'Now lad. Have you broken that computer again?'

'No sir,' Ahmed protested.

'Well, what do you want?'

'I've got an e-mail from ballistics, sir. I know you'd want to see it straight away.' He passed the paper over the desk.

Angel folded the newspaper, tossed it on a chair and took the e-mail eagerly.

'Ta. Where's Crisp?'

'Don't know, sir. I can try to raise him on his mobile.'

'Ay. Do that, lad.'

Ahmed turned to go.

'Hang on. Have you read this?'

'Yes, sir.'

'Mmm.'

It read:

<u>History on Walther PPK/S No. A22394297WT.</u>

Manufactured in 1969. Originally sold to Dutch police, one of a batch of 40. The Dutch police do not say how or when it left their possession.

It was recovered by Royal Ulster Constabulary in July 1984 following a bank raid in Belfast and despatched to an RAOC ordnance depot in North Yorkshire. It was stolen from there overnight between 21 August 1985 and 22 August 1985.

Two of the three robbers were caught, tried in Lincoln and jailed, but part of the haul including the gun was not recovered.

The robbers were Alan Gledhill Taylor (aka Alan Fields and Jonno Fields) aged 38 and Peter Patrick Stone aged 22.

Angel looked up. He scratched his chin.

'Mm. Ahmed. I've got a little job for you.' He handed the

e-mail back to him. 'Print out their photographs. And find out their known associates. Straight away.'

Ahmed took the paper. 'Right, sir.'

There was a knock at the door.

Ahmed opened it. It was DS Crisp.

'Come in, lad. Where've you been? I've been looking all over for you. Been squeezing your boil?'

'I haven't got a boil.'

'I should hope not.'

Angel noticed the young cadet smirking.

'Hurry up with that job, Cadet,' he yelled. 'I've something else I want you to do when you come back.' He turned to Crisp. 'Now sit down, Sergeant.'

The door closed.

Angel opened the desk drawer and found a see-through evidence bag in which he had put the remains of the broken plastic tube-shaped container.

'I want you to take this to Mac at the hospital. He's expecting it.'

'What is it, sir?'

'I don't know. I found it round the rubbish at Eric Weltham's place. I am hoping Mac will be able to tell me. What's it look like to you?'

'A broken plastic container. Could be from a child's chemistry set or similar.'

'Ay. Could be, I suppose. When you've delivered it, I want you to find someone for me.'

Crisp dipped into his pocket for his notebook.

'A missing person, sir?'

'No. A woman aged about sixty-five. Small, thin, weight about seven stone or less, white hair, known as "Mrs Tassel". I presume resident locally.'

Crisp looked up from his notebook.

'Not much to go on, sir.'

Angel smiled, but he wasn't pleased.

'Would it help if I gave you her car registration number?' He pulled out his own notebook and showed Crisp the number.

The sergeant silently copied it into his own book.

'Do you want me to bring her in?'

Angel frowned. 'No, lad. No. Just find out what you can about her, covertly. That's all.'

'Right, sir.'

Crisp went out as Ahmed came in.

'Now then? Have you got those pictures? Any Roger Moores among them?'

Ahmed gave the inspector print-outs of the head-and-shoulder photographs of two ugly men with hair shaved to the scalp. Angel glanced at them.

'Hmm. No, there isn't,' he said, answering his own question. 'Mmm. Don't know either of them. Hmm. Have you got that list of associates?'

'Yes sir. There are six.'

'Ta, lad.' Angel stuck his head into the list of names. 'Mmm.' Suddenly he looked up at Ahmed. 'Here's one, lad.' He read it out loud. 'Angus Stuart Holmes (aka Robert Birch, aka Alan McFee) Born Glasgow Royal Free Hospital, first January 1935. Died twentieth August 1990, Helensburgh, aged fifty-five.' He looked up, his eyes shining. 'Mmm. That was in 1990. He was the father of Irish John Holmes. Now we are getting somewhere. Mmm. I must get to see him.' He turned to Ahmed. 'I've another job for you, lad. It'll take you out of the office.'

Ahmed beamed. Angel noticed he was pleased. It would make a change from logging in statistics.

'It's not an excuse for mucking about, lad.'

'No, sir.'

'Ay. Well, do you know what a carnation flower looks like?'

'Of course I do, sir. They wear them at weddings in lapels and that.'

'Ay. I want you to go round all the florists' shops in Bromersley. And I mean *all*. I reckon there'll be about six or eight. Anyway, look in Yellow Pages.'

'Yes sir.'

'Find out if there's a shop that has in the last two weeks, sold a single pink carnation for use as a buttonhole. I think a florist might remember that. Then see if they can tell you who bought it, or describe them to you.'

Ahmed nodded knowingly. 'Like the one worn by the Man in Pink?'

'That's right, lad. Exactly. But don't prompt them, you understand?'

'Yes sir.' He turned to the door.

'I'm going up the Mawdsley Estate,' Angel said. 'You can get me on my mobile if anything crops up.'

'Right sir.'

Angel pointed his car north out of town. He was going to seek out Irish John Holmes. He needed to confirm that Irish John's father had given him the stolen gun before he died, and that Irish John had sold it to Jones. That's the sort of evidence the CPS's barrister would sell his mother for; the case against Jones was strong, but more supporting evidence would not be unwelcome.

Angel turned out of the police station yard into Market Street then into Market Hill. Out of his eye corner he saw a striking young woman leap out of a brand-new burgundy-coloured Jaguar limousine parked outside the Northern Bank. He had to drive carefully; the road was busy. His eyes zipped back to look more closely at the long legged brunette. She was

THE MAN IN THE PINK SUIT

wearing a short astrakhan coat with the collar turned up and she was carrying a black leather handbag. She looked round as she pulled the key out of the car door. She needn't have bothered: everybody *was* looking at her. She had not gone unnoticed by all the male populace over fifteen.

A tall tanned young man held the glass door of the bank open for her and was rewarded with a big carmine smile and a dimple. Angel suddenly realized who it was. It was Ingrid Dooley. Wow! she had certainly come out of herself since he had first met her at Charles Tabor's factory five days ago. She had looked attractive then, but not eye-dazzling as she unquestionably was this afternoon.

He was certain he had seen her somewhere before, but he couldn't place where. One day something would trigger his memory and it would all coming flooding back. The more he thought about her, the more he knew he needed to ask her some very pointed questions.

Ingrid Dooley passed out of his mind as he pressed the car towards the Mawdsley Estate. He was heading for the little shop where Irish John Holmes lived with Kathleen Docherty and their son. He was still considering how he might approach the subject of the Walther his father had stolen in 1990. Irish John was no pushover. He wasn't bright, but he was bright enough not to incriminate himself. It wasn't going to be easy to get him to tell him the truth.

He was considering this as he turned into Market Street and was passing the local hotel: The Feathers. His attention was suddenly caught by the erratic antics in the pub doorway of a tall thin man with a small head, who was hanging uncertainly on to a well-dressed, long-legged girl wearing a tight black sweater, a navy-blue coat and red skirt. The man was wearing an ill-fitting suit, a white silk scarf and an ancient trilby, and he was waving a hand about as if he was conducting the Hallé Orchestra. Then he seemed to lose his balance. He turned to reach out to the door jamb, missed and fell. The girl tried to save him but he fell on to the pavement on his back- side. He nearly pulled the girl down on top of him, but she unravelled herself from him in time and now stood there staring down at him. He sat there a few moments looking up at her and laughing. He was clearly drunk.

Angel recognized him straight away. It was Irish John, the man he was on his way to see. He didn't know the girl, but for certain it was not Kathleen Docherty, the woman John had said he was going to marry. Angel stopped the car and pulled over to the kerb. He looked back to the hotel. A few passers- by were trying not to notice the drunk still sitting in the hotel entrance. Irish John fumbled round for his hat, found it and slapped it unceremoniously on his head. Then he looked up at the girl, smiled and held his arms up to her. She was also laughing. She took his hands and after a struggle managed to get him to his feet. Then she wrapped her arms round him to keep him standing upright.

Angel had an idea. He reached for his mobile phone and tapped in a number.

'Hello, Crisp? ... I'm outside The Feathers. I'm observing Irish John Holmes and a woman, and I want you to come down here and take over from me straight away. It's the woman I want to know about, lad. Hurry up!'

Inspector Angel pulled up his car outside 11 Westbourne Grove, a small modern bungalow in the better residential area of Bromersley. He crossed the pavement, pushed open the little wrought-iron gate and made his way up the short path to the glass-panelled front door. He pressed the illuminated button set on the door jamb, heard the ding, and waited staring at the modern bubble-patterned glass panel patiently.

The door was presently opened a little way by a small elderly woman with grey hair. Angel was pleased to see that it was the driver of the car he had followed from Eric Weltham's house the day before. So far so good.

'Yes?' she asked peering and blinking through the mean gap the doorchain would allow.

Angel smiled. 'Is it Mrs Tassel?'

'Yes,' she said with an enquiring smile, surprised to be addressed by name by a stranger.

'I'm Inspector Angel of the Bromersley Police. Might I have a few words?'

'Well – erm. What's it about?' she said nervously.

Angel pursed his lips. 'Well, it's a bit difficult to talk to you out here.'

'Oh.'

Angel took out his wallet and held up his warrant card for her to see it through the gap.

'There you are. Can you see it?' He pointed to the photograph. 'That there isn't a monkey.'

She looked at him curiously.

'It's me,' he added with a smile.

She looked at the photograph, grinned and unfastened the door latch.

'Come in. Go straight ahead, turn left into the front room. I've got the heater on in there. I'm busy doing some sewing for a customer.' She closed the front door and followed him down the hallway.

'Thank you,' Angel said, pushing open the door.

The little room was clearly dedicated to sewing. There was a three-piece suite pushed against a wall, a table in the middle of the floor and a heavy duty sewing-machine next to it.

'Sit down,' she said as she closed the room door and pointed at the nearest easy chair. 'Oh, I'll just move these skirts.'

She swept the skirts off the chair and dumped them on the table. She took up position on the chair in front of the sewing-machine with her back to a small electric fire in the grate.

Angel relaxed into the big easy-chair positioned against the wall.

'So you're a dressmaker, Mrs Tassel?' he said breezily, trying to put her at ease.

'A widow has to make a living somehow, Inspector,' she said with a ready smile.

'Indeed. What sort of dresses do you make?'

'I don't make many dresses. A few garments for young girls now and then. So far as sewing for women is concerned, most of the work I do is letting clothes out or taking them in.' She pointed to the skirts on the table. 'I am about to take those waistbands in. About six weeks ago, I was letting them out for her. It's a customer who has a weight problem. She's up and down like a yoyo.'

'Bulimic?'

'No. I don't think so. She's in showbusiness and she always has to look good in front of the cameras. She has a huge wardrobe and finds it difficult to keep her weight down. She's either on a strict diet or she's bingeing.'

'Mmm.' Angel nodded. 'Must be Miss Louella Panter.'

Mrs Tasell looked surprised. 'Er – yes.'

'Do you make clothes for men?' he asked quickly.

'Yes.

'Do you make suits?'

'Yes.'

'Have you ever made a pink suit?'

Mrs Tassel had a very nice smile. She beamed across at him. 'You're joshing me.'

'No, Mrs Tassel. I'm serious.'

'No, of course not. A pink suit, never. I have made men's

and boys' suits in all kinds of materials, colours and shades but never pink. I made a beautiful two-piece alpaca suit for a gentleman only last week. It was in cream. The idea!'

'There's a chap on the telly who wears a pink suit,' Angel prompted.

Her eyes shone briefly.

'So there is.' She stuck her nose up and said: 'Well, I wouldn't make any clothes for *him* under any circumstances. That's that man, Frank P. Jones you're referring to, isn't it? And doesn't he look ridiculous in sunglasses and a straw hat in midwinter?' She shook her and pouted. 'He shot a man didn't he?'

Angel nodded. 'I'm trying to find out who makes his suits.'

'Oh, *that*'s what brings you here?'

'Yes.'

'Well I have no idea who makes those ridiculous suits for him. And I hope that Mr Jones goes to prison for a very long time.'

Angel was taken aback by her vehemence.

'Do you know the man, then?'

'I've met him. It was his fault a gentleman I know – knew, he's dead now – had to give up the violin. In fact, his daughter Ingrid always said that it was that that killed him.'

'What's that?' Angel raised an eyebrow. 'His daughter Ingrid?'

'She works at the factory where it all happened. Ingrid Dooley. A nice lass. You must have come across her. She's quite a looker now. She's done very well for herself since her father died. Don't know why she never got married.'

'I've met her, yes,' Angel said, trying to look uninterested. He leaned back in the easy-chair and nodded encouragingly.

Mrs Tassel waved a finger for emphasis.

'Well her father was a first violinist when I was a second.

We were with the same agency, so we often played at the same concerts and things, accompanying choirs and soloists and so on. Anyway, there was a big do at a town hall near Leeds. I had just arrived. Alec Dooley was already there. So was Frank Jones. He was the announcer, compère or whatever they call them these days. He and the director were talking. They seemed to have had an argument and he then stormed off the stage. On his way to his dressing-room, he brushed past a trolley of instruments and music stands and knocked them over. Mr Dooley's violin was among the pile so naturally, he rescued it and opened the case to see that it wasn't damaged, then he went into Jones's dressing-room to tell him off. Jones wasn't at all apologetic. Instead he told him to get out and pushed Alec, who was only a little man, towards the door. Alec lost his balance and landed on the floor. He put his hands out in front to save himself and the violin and in the process broke his wrist.

'I went with him to the hospital in Leeds. It was a bad break. A collis fracture I think they call it. Jones never apologized or offered to pay or anything. Alec was in plaster for six weeks. He never played again. In fact, I always said it was the beginning of the end for him. Indeed it was. He died on Christmas Day two years ago.'

Angel left Mrs Tassel not altogether satisfied with the interview. All he seemed to have discovered was that Ingrid Dooley had a strong reason to dislike Frank P Jones. He wondered how that fact fitted into the puzzle. He was of the opinion that Ingrid had not been entirely frank with him, and he still couldn't put his finger on where he had met her before. It was annoying him. He went straight home.

As it was Friday, his wife Mary had cooked finny haddock for their tea. He watched a bit of television and went to bed. It had been a difficult day. The ultimatum from Superintendent Harker had now expired. Come Monday, he would have to push the Jones case into court whether it was ready or not. There was such a lot to attend to do. He slept the sleep of the just and woke at six o'clock as fresh as the frost on his lawn.

He started early. He left home at 7 a.m., went to the office to clear some of the outstanding post and then at 8.30 a.m. drove straight up to the Mawdsley estate. He pulled up outside the little shop run by Kathleen Docherty and where Irish John and their little boy Liam lived. There were no customers in the little shop; Kathleen was doing what she always seemed to be doing: stacking bread into shelves to make more room. She looked up from behind the counter.

'Oh it's you again, Inspectour,' she said unnecessarily loudly in a hard Belfast twang. 'Inspectour Angel, isn't it? How are you, Inspectour?'

Angel heard a door close somewhere behind her. Without a word, he nipped smartly out of the shop and turned into the ginnel. He ran down to the end in time to see Irish John straddled across the wooden fence that marked off the extent of the tiny, forsaken garden from the field beyond.

'Just the man I wanted to see,' Angel called out.

'Oh? I'll be coming back to you then, Inspector.'

Irish John cocked his leg back over the fence. He was wearing his suit and old trilby and, unusually, a collar and tie.

'I was just laving. I was taking a short cut. I was going to … er … er—'

'Work?'

The man smiled. 'I cannot tell a loy, Inspector. I don't have a job yet. It isn't easy to get work when you've just come out, you know. I was just on my way to see about a job, though. I was hoping to get an interview tomorrow.' He nodded enthusiastically.

He came up to Angel who was standing by the back door.

'Tomorrow's Sunday.' Angel said lightly.

Irish John smiled again. 'Yus. Or next week.'

'Well, I won't hold you up, John. Just a few questions. I wouldn't want to hinder your getting work. I know how eager you are to get back into employment.'

John came up very close to the inspector and spoke in a soft voice with one eye on the backdoor.

'To tell you the trute, it's Kathleen that wants me to get a full-time job. I would be happy enough helping her in the shop, and delivering orders and that, but no, she wants me to get a nine-to-five job with a regular income and a pension. A proper job, she says, like her brother. He works in the ship-yard, you know. A foreman. Yus. Well, when I came out, I thought she'd want me near her. You know. All the time. And keeping an eye on Liam. I can play wid him. And keep him out of mischief. But she says she wants me to get a job so that she knows where I am. When I was in Strangeways, she says, I was no help to her there, but at least she knew where I was. There's no understanding women, Inspector Angel, is there. I mean, we are supposed to be getting married next month. You'd think she would be wanting me to be by her side, wouldn't you now?'

Angel sighed and then smiled, then he thought of Irish John with that woman in the short red skirt, drunk on the pavement outside The Feathers yesterday and considered what a shifty, oily little toad he was. Some Romeo. Looked as if Kathleen Docherty was a suitable match for this little man. She was certainly big enough and intelligent enough to handle herself in an even contest with him.

Irish John came closer. 'She's with chile, you know,' he said, in a quiet voice. 'We're going to have another. A friend for Liam. So very soon we are planning to tie the knot, that we are.' He nodded with a smile. Then he added, sensitively: 'I'm really very fond of her, you know, Inspector.'

Angel was in a situation rare for him: he didn't know what to say. He pulled away from the man's warm nicotine-laden breath.

'I intend to do right by her,' John continued with several nods. 'For better or for worse.'

Angel wanted to press on. 'I'll leave you to settle your love life, lad. I want to ask you about your father.'

John licked his lips and then looked down and shook his head slowly.

'He's passed on you know, a while ago now.'

'I know.' Irish John nodded, paused, then, looking up to the sky, said: 'A good man, gone to meet his Maker.'

'He was a liar and a thief and a conman,' said Angel.

'True, true,' Irish John said without flinching. 'But he was a good father to me. He was responsible for teaching me all I know. He died in a convent in County Donegal surrounded by the nuns. They were praying for him. You see, he'd repented for all his mistakes and the priest there had given him absolution. He had taken to doing all sorts of work around the old building. He rewired the place for electricity, and put in a central heating-system for the old mother superior who had the arthritis on her knees. It was all that praying, you know. Yes. Mmm. He had done all sorts of jobs for them since his conversion.'

Angel shook his head, rubbed his chin and said, 'Have you any onions?'

John's jaw dropped momentarily and then he said busily:

'Yes, sor. I'm sure Kathleen's got some in the shop. What do you want? A pound? Two pounds?'

'Oh, they're not for me, John.'

'Oh?'

'For you, lad.'

'For me?'

'Yes. To go with that tripe you've just handed out. Put the onions with it and you'll have a lovely panful of tripe and onions.'

John gave him a long, slow look, his mouth slightly open.

Angel shook his head.

The man licked his lips and then smiled.

'You're joshing me, Inspector. You're joshing me. You knew I was kidding you, didn't you?'

Angel gave him a straight look.

'Your father died on the twentieth of August, 1990, aged fifty-five, up in Scotland, a place called Helensburgh,' he said reproachfully.

'That's roight. That's roight. My, you are well informed this morning, Inspector.'

'Oh I'm always well informed, John. You should know that.'

Irish John beamed and nodded.

'Oh yes. There's not much gets past you, Mr Angel,' he said slyly in that slow, soft imitation Irish drawl he had perfected.

'Yes. That's right. And you see I happen to know what you were up to yesterday afternoon.'

'Let me see, now where was I?'

'Between three o'clock and four.'

'I was here.'

'No you weren't.'

'I was here!'

'No.'

'Kathleen will tell you. I was here.'

'No. I know exactly where you were and who you were with.'

There was a pause.

'Ah!' Irish John said as the penny dropped. His mouth froze

in the open position. His eyes moved across their sockets twice before coming to rest on Angel's beaming face eight inches from his nose.

Irish John moved back a step. He licked his lips and then consciously changed the shape of them into a smile.

Angel nodded slowly. Irish John looked towards the house door and then back.

'Mmm. You wouldn't be wanting to spread it around would you, Mr Angel?'

'No,' Angel lied, knowing full well that Irish John knew he was lying. 'It's not important,' he went on. 'What is important is what you did with the Walther PPK/S 32 that your father gave you just before he died.'

TEN

Detective Inspector Michael Angel stood in his vest and pants, in front of the mirror in the bathroom in his bungalow on the edge of the South Yorkshire town of Bromersley. The transistor radio on the window ledge was banging out a racket made with guitars and drums interspersed with a fast-talking obsequious man who stumbled through tit-bits of vital local news, about a man who had fallen off his bicycle in the High Street, a woman who collected used bus tickets and an interview with a boy genius, who had a conker that was a twenty-niner.

Angel didn't hear what the DJ man was saying. He had too much on his mind. He was thinking that tomorrow morning, he would have to parcel the case, *Regina v. Jones* and push it up to the CPS. The superintendent was certain to arrange a special sitting of the magistrates' court to put the man in the pink suit on remand in his absence, and therefore, out of the jurisdiction of Bromersley police. If he did that, Angel knew he would not be able to question him even informally and, unravelling the truth in the case would become much more difficult.

He was about to apply shaving foam to his face when he stopped and stared closely into the glass. He was attracted to the handsome face, the thick shock of shiny dark hair and the blue eyes, and he wondered if there really *had* been any improvement since he had given up the fags and the booze. After he had grimaced and pouted several times, to tighten the skin, he snarled at the mirror and made a decision: there was nothing for it, he would have to give up pork pies and chips as well!

He applied the soap and was about to make the first stroke down his cheek with the razor, when it happened. Ping! It came to him like a flash of lightning. It came from nowhere. He suddenly knew where he had seen Ingrid Dooley before. The scene came flooding back like a three-second film-strip. He could see her in the waiting-room at the police station, wiping tears from her eyes with his handkerchief. He was delighted that his memory had at last spewed out the little scene from a year or two back. He was impatient to get to work the following morning, so that he could arrange to see Ingrid Dooley, and, at the same time, try to keep out of the way of the superintendent.

The morning of a new week came soon enough, and as he drove rapidly past the front of Bromersley police station, he was pleased to note that the media circus of TV vans and cars, and the skate-board boys had gone and he wondered what sort of a commotion there would be outside Bromersley General Hospital. He turned into the station yard and made for his office.

As he was unfastening the buttons of his raincoat, he glanced across at the high pile of fresh post delivered to the in-tray, and growled something that sounded like 'sugar', but was not as sweet.

Ahmed knocked on the open door and came in with his head down carrying another handful of letters.

Angel pulled up the swivel chair and dropped into it. He took an envelope out of his pocket on which he had made some notes over the weekend and consulted them.

The young cadet silently packed the letters safely into the in-tray. Then he remained standing in front of the desk. He looked first at the inspector then down at his feet. There was clearly something wrong. His face was not its usual smiling self. He didn't make any effort to leave. Angel sensed something was wrong and looked up.

'What is it, lad? Not been taking your syrup of figs?'

'No sir,' he muttered.

'Just made your last will and testament?'

'No sir.'

Angel sighed and shook his head.

'Well, are you going to tell me, or do I have to guess best of three?'

Ahmed looked up. 'Erm … no sir. On Saturday, I went all round the town, sir. I haven't missed a single florist's shop. I've even been in greengrocers that *might* have sold flowers, and *nobody* has asked for a pink carnation on its own in the last fortnight.'

Angel smiled across at the small sad face.

'Right lad. That's all right then.'

Ahmed's mouth opened. 'That's all right, sir?'

'If you're sure you've not missed anybody.'

'Oh no,' said Ahmed decisively. 'I haven't missed anybody.'

'Right then.'

Ahmed smiled broadly.

Angel nodded. 'I've got another job for you. In fact I've got several.'

The young man looked like a hundred-yards sprinter on starting-blocks.

'What sir? What?'

'First. I want you to run through that videotape of Jones and find me all the frames showing his face full front that you can. There aren't many, I know. He's wearing a hat and sunglasses, but the best you can find. Then blow them up as far as they'll go, print them off and bring them in. All right?'

Ahmed nodded.

'Then I want you to find out who is on duty at the hospital and find out from him how Jones is, and let me know. Then I want you to get me DS Gawber on the phone. He'll be at home.'

'Yes sir.'

Ahmed started counting on his fingers.

'Then I want you to find DS Crisp, he should be at Jones's house, I expect with Dr Mac. I want him back here pronto.

'Then I want you go back in the records, and see what you can find out about a man called Dooley. He died in the street outside Pewski's the undertakers on Sheffield Road about two years ago. His daughter is Ingrid Dooley.'

Ahmed's face lit up. 'Anything else, sir?'

'No.'

Ahmed made for the door. 'Right sir.'

'Yes,' Angel called after him. 'Make us a cup of tea. Now. And hurry up.'

The young cadet dashed out of the office.

Angel looked after him, shook his head and smiled. Then he reached over to the in-tray, began unloading it and groaned.

The telephone rang.

'Angel.' It was the girl on the switchboard. 'There's a person-to-person call to you from California in America. Couldn't get the name of the caller.'

He frowned. 'America? California?'

'That's what he said, Inspector.'

'Right. Put him on.'

There was a click.

'Detective Inspector Angel speaking. Who is that?'

A very loud American voice came over the line.

'This is Hiram P Zabonski of Epic Film Studios, Hollywood. Is that Michael Angel, chief of homicide?'

'Yes. I suppose so.'

'The detective investigating the Man in the Pink Suit inquiry?'

'Yes, sir. What can I do for you?'

'Ah. I'm very pleased to speak with you, sir. We've heard of you, Michael, here in Hollywood, and what a top-notch job you are doing in the inquiry. And I'd like to offer you a starring part in a movie we are going to start shooting over here in three or four weeks' time.'

Angel's jaw dropped. 'I think there must be some mistake.'

'No. No. There's no mistake. I've seen you on the English take of CNN news. You have a very magnetic personality, Michael. The sort audiences like. Now what I'm proposing is a contract for ten thousand dollars a week, ten weeks minimum.'

Angel grinned then shook his head.

'Oh? Erm ... I'm a policeman. I can't just drop everything.'

'I know. I know. But this is the offer of a lifetime, Michael. This film would put you up there with such greats, like Peter Falk and Raymond Burr. Don't worry about any contractual employment contracts you may have with the English police. We will buy them out. Won't cost you a penny. All you have to do is pack a bag and get on a plane here. We'll pay the fare. I can have the fare telegraphed to you today. You'll get it in the morning. Are you married?'

'Yes.'

'You can bring your wife too. That's OK.'

'I can't do *that*.'

'Why not?'

'I can't. What's the part? What's the film about, anyway?'

'It's a great screenplay. Great. You'll love it. It's about the Man in the Pink Suit who shoots a man in broad daylight and gets away with it.'

Angel pulled a face. '*How* does he get away with it?'

'We don't know *that*, Michael. The story isn't played out yet, is it?'

'Oh?' Angel was nonplussed.

'Your role is that of the detective, of course. I want you to replay *exactly* the part you have been playing since Frank P. Jones shot this computer mogul. It's powerful drama!'

Angel sighed. 'No. I couldn't do that.'

'It'll be a superb script. I've got the six best writers in the world working on it. It's a terrific part for you. Why not?'

Angel wasn't going to America for ten weeks, he knew that.

There was a short silence, Angel said: 'I'm sorry, but I can't.'

'I'll tell you what, Michael,' the American continued louder than ever. 'Let's make it *twenty* thousand dollars a week with a minimum of ten weeks and a contract for another movie. How's that?'

'It's not the money, Mr ... er.'

'Hiram. Call me Hiram.'

'It's not the money, Hiram. I just can't come to America. I can't leave here just now.'

'It's a great opportunity for you, Michael. We'll be coming over there later, to shoot some exteriors in your beautiful York Shire.'

'No thanks. I've *got* a job. I've got a murder to solve. I'm sorry.'

'What if I come over there and—'

'No. No. Don't do that. Thanks for the offer, but no thanks. No thanks.'

He replaced the receiver on the cradle. He took a deep breath, smiled and wondered whether he had missed the opportunity of a lifetime. The more he thought about it, the more he came to the conclusion he hadn't. And his wife Mary wouldn't have moved out of Bromersley even if Hiram had offered her a solid gold kitchen, a diamond studded oven and a flock of trained flunkeys.

There was a knock on the door.

'Come in!'

It was Ahmed with a cup of tea. He carried it precariously on a black tin tray advertising the merits of Bromersley Best Bitter.

'I've phoned the hospital and I have spoken to Constable Scrivens, sir.'

Angel looked up. 'Ah yes?'

'He said that it was a bit of a bear garden. He had to chase television people and autograph hunters out of the ward. But all's well now. He said Mr Jones seems to have had a quiet night. He doesn't look much different from when he went in. He is still sleeping a lot. He is still on a drip and still wearing an oxygen mask. The doctors haven't been round to see him yet. He thinks he must be sedated.'

Angel looked up. 'Sedated?'

'Yes sir. That's what he said.'

Angel ran his hand strongly round his mouth and jaw.

'Did you manage to get Sergeant Gawber?'

'I'll get him now for you, if you like.'

'Ay.'

Ahmed dialled the number. Angel thoughtfully sipped the tea. As the dialling tone rang out, the young man said:

'Sounds as if Mr Jones is very ill, sir.'

'Ay, lad, it does.'

'What would happen if he died, sir?'

Angel shook his head, considered the question briefly.

'I reckon if he died, lad, it would be murder.'

Ahmed's eyes shone like a cat's caught in headlights.

'Murder?' he muttered.

There was the sound of a click and a voice from the earpiece.

Ahmed passed the handset to Angel and made for the door. The Inspector waved him back.

'Is that Ron Gawber?'

'Yes. Oh. Good morning sir.'

'How's the ankle?'

'Painful.'

'Can you walk?'

'With difficulty, sir. On crutches, you know.'

'Ron, do you think you could do a bit of guard duty at the hospital? I've got Frank P Jones in there. It's a sit down job. You could take a book. The place is surrounded with media. I am worried about his security.'

There was hesitation.

'Yes. All right sir. I'm bored here anyway.'

'That's great. Thanks Ron. I'll send the area car.'

He replaced the phone and turned to Ahmed.

'Tell the desk sergeant I want a car to transport DS Gawber to the hospital pronto.'

'Yes sir. Pronto.'

'Did you get hold of DS Crisp?'

'He's on his way, sir,' Ahmed said, his hand on the doorknob.

'Good lad.'

The door closed.

Angel reached out to the in-tray and filtered through the pile looking for one particular packet. He found it. It was an A5 manila envelope, personally addressed to him, with the words: Star Agencies, Personal Management, Charing Cross Road, London, printed on the flap. He opened it carefully with a penknife and slid out a ten-inch-by-eight-inch photograph mounted on cream board and covered with tissue, together with a With Compliments slip. It had a note scrawled on the slip in big writing, *Photo as requested*, and it was simply signed *Jack Starr*. The caption under the photograph read: Frank P Jones, studying a cartoon by Leonardo da Vinci, in the Louvre, Paris, June 2004. The picture was almost a full-square front view of Jones, from the top of his straw hat down to his shoes, in his pink suit, carnation, bow tie, shoes, the lot. He was holding the da Vinci framed drawing with his right hand and signalling with his left, looking in the camera, in one of his flamboyant, royal-type gestures.

Angel reckoned it was an excellent photograph of Jones, a good representation of the man, faithful in colour and sharp in focus, and he murmured his satisfaction.

There was a knock at the door.

'Come in.'

It was DS Crisp. 'You wanted me, sir?'

'Yes.' Angel put the photograph down. 'I thought you were going through Jones's house with Mac.'

'I was. We finished last night, sir.'

'Oh. Anything new?'

'No sir. Nothing.'

'Any drugs, cash, gold, firearms, explosives, pornography, a hidden safe?'

'No sir. Nothing like that.'

Angel raised his eyebrows. 'That's a surprise.' He glared at Crisp and added: 'I hope you looked! Has Mac taken his pink suit and stuff to the lab?'

'Yes sir. He says he'll let you have the entire outfit tomorrow.'

'Ay.' Angel rubbed his chin with his hand. He thought tomorrow might be too late. He picked up the photograph. 'Take a look at this, lad.'

Crisp took it and eagerly peeled back the tissue, carefully avoiding touching the surface with his fingers.

'Yes,' he said appreciatively. 'Very nice, sir.' He turned it over. 'Has he autographed it?'

Angel scowled and tightened his grip on the chair arms.

'Autographed it?' he roared. 'This isn't *Top of the Pops*! He

THE MAN IN THE PINK SUIT

snatched the photograph back. 'This a murder case, lad. We're not running a fan club! This isn't pop memorabilia!'

Crisp made his lips the shape of a doughnut and exhaled slowly. He said nothing.

Angel shoved the photograph back into its envelope and pushed it roughly into Crisp's hand.

'Here. Take it. I want you to pick up the statements of those four women who work at Tabor's factory. Cadet Ahaz has them. Then go up there and interview them each in turn *again*. That secretary lass, Ingrid Dooley, might let you borrow her office for the job. She's a bit of a looker, but keep away. She's spoken for. I know you think you're a bit of a ladies' man, but she could gobble you up and spit out the bones to make soup for Maggie Thatcher!' He pointed to the envelope. '*That* is the latest photograph of Jones,' he said. 'Take care of it. And I want it back. Ask those women whether they are positive he is the man who shot Charles Tabor. The slightest difference. Anything. They must speak now. I want a firm yea or nay. Their evidence is absolutely vital. They'll be called into the box, and I don't want any muck ups in front of the judge. All right?'

'Right, sir.'

'And another thing. You know a hundred thousand pounds has gone walkabout out of that safe up there. It reportedly went missing between four and five o'clock the afternoon of Tabor's murder. See what alibis those girls can provide for themselves for that time slot. See if they know anything at all about the robbery. Jones denies taking it. Well, we know *he* didn't go near the safe, the videotapes tell us that. Ask again if they saw anybody anywhere near the safe that day. The slightest clue. Fish about. Use your initiative. You know what to do.' He sighed. 'We have nothing to go on at all!'

*

It was 9 a.m. Another day, and forty-eight hours past the deadline the superintendent had given Angel to wrap up the Jones case and pass it on to the CPS. Angel was only too well aware of this and he was still managing to keep out of the super's way. He was waiting for the forensic report from Mac about Jones's house and the pink suit and then he would have to make a decision. In the meantime, this morning, he was looking for £100,000 and the place he hoped to find it was at 455 Sheffield Road, the home of Eric Weltham, MP.

He drove along Sheffield Road, past the posh flats, to Weltham's house. The American car was not there. A big black car was parked in its place, and there was a man in the driver's seat wearing a nebbed hat pushed to the back of his head. He was smoking a cigarette and reading the *Guardian*. That looked like a cabinet minister's car; perhaps Louella and Nigel were off somewhere. Angel got out his car and strode determinedly up the path carrying a fawn coloured paper file.

It was Eric Weltham himself who answered the door. He looked very smart in a broad pin-striped dark suit. He scowled when he saw it was Angel.

'What do you want, Inspector?' he growled.

Angel spoke forthrightly, not rude, but in that no-nonsense style that is supposed to epitomize the Yorkshire character.

'A few questions, sir. It will take only three minutes.'

'Make it two and I'll see you now. Otherwise you'll have to make an appointment in London with my secretary. I have to be off. My car is waiting.'

'I can ask the questions in ten seconds, sir. It really depends on you how long you take to answer them.'

Weltham growled, then he snapped, 'Come in.' He showed Angel into a dark wood-panelled room with shelves of books covering most of the wall space, a French window, a few chairs, and a big desk in the centre of the room. He pointed

Angel to a chair and took another himself behind the desk.

'Now what is it,' he said testily, looking at his watch.

Angel opened the folder, it held only a single sheet of A4 paper, handwritten on both sides. He glanced at the sheet, turned it over and then silently read a few lines. He closed the file and looked across the desk.

'I have a statement here from a witness who overheard you and Charles Tabor discussing competitors' tenders for computers for the R and D ministry and an arrangement whereby you supplied details of the tenders in return for a cash payment to you of a hundred thousand pounds.'

Weltham pouted. 'Ridiculous. Outrageous!' he bellowed.

Unmoved, Angel said coolly: 'I wondered if you had anything to say to rebut the statement.' He placed the file on the polished desk.

'Oh yes. Yes. I've plenty to say,' roared Weltham. 'Plenty. I deny it absolutely. It's complete nonsense. Who is it that libels me in this way? Who is it? I'll sue them for every penny they've got. A bit of tittle-tattle does not constitute a case to bring against me, an MP, a cabinet minister and a member of Her Majesty's Privy Council. Whoever it is had better have a super abundance of evidence and a damn good counsel to deliver it. I can tell you that. Who is it?'

'I am not at liberty to say, sir.'

'I thought you'd say that. Where was it? And when?'

'Your counsel will be informed of that in due course.'

'Oh yes? You definitely intend bringing it to court, then?'

'In the absence of some satisfactory explanation, I have no option, sir.'

Weltham bit his lip. He wished he hadn't. He regretted letting Angel see how much this charge was unnerving him. There was a short pause. He stood up and went over to the french windows, he put his hands in his pockets and looked out across the garden at the long lawn and the greenhouses, but he didn't see them. He soon recovered his composure and returned to the desk rubbing his chin. He sat down, leaned forward and looked straight into Angel's eyes.

'Well now, Inspector,' he said in a low measured voice, 'it seems to me that you have got yourself in a bit of a pickle.'

'How's that, sir?' Angel said, wondering what was coming next.

'You have got the wrong side of me for a start,' said Weltham icily. 'This trumped-up story is typical of the way my political enemies try to bring me down. It's a device. A politician's life is a minefield. Your informant, whoever he is, will not be a man of substance and he will not find anybody of standing to support his story. There is nobody in the world who can make this sort of fairy-tale stick with unsupported evidence. And you haven't got any or you wouldn't be sitting here now trying to bluff me into a confession. And I think you are a wise enough bird to know that what I say is true. Litigation against me could run into several millions. No prosecution barrister in his right mind would touch the case. So if you decide to take this fabricated claptrap to court, if you are stupid enough, not only would you inevitably lose the case, but you would lose your credibility and in turn, probably your job!'

Weltham was cleverer than Angel had thought. Most of what the man had said was true. He knew he'd never get a case to stick on present evidence, but he was not beaten yet. He intended to fight this battle to the end. He sat there waiting for Weltham to finish his spiel.

'On the other hand, I have noticed what a hard-working, determined, single-minded, go-ahead man you are. And you are your own man; I like that. Now, as it happens, one of my best front-bench friends and colleagues is the Home Secretary, Sir Jasper Keene. He listens to me, Inspector. And he owes me a favour. Now if you could see your way clear – in view of the hopelessness of the case – to dropping it, and say, losing that statement, I would whisper a few words in his ear, and I don't see why you shouldn't be a superintendent ... in a few weeks' time.'

Angel's face changed. He was sickened at what he had heard and he slowly shook his head.

'That won't do, sir,' he said quietly. 'That won't do at all. I know you are guilty of accepting money by using your high office for your own ends. And I'm going to do all that I can to get you to pay for it. I am not beaten yet. As for trying to bribe me, well, I don't think I have ever thought of being a superintendent. It's not really my cup of tea. I really don't want the responsibility of being in charge of CID: all that paperwork and meetings. I enjoy my job as inspector. It's not too low, and it's not too high. I don't mind getting my hands dirty occasionally chasing leeches like you and locking them up.'

He stood up. His pulse was banging away in his ears. His face was red. He had a hot pain in his chest that he always experienced when his gander was up. 'I do regret that in this case,' he went on, 'It will take me a little longer.' He reached out in front to pick up the file and instead knocked it flying across the top of the polished desk. The inside sheet slid out right in front of Weltham's nose.

'Give me that here,' Angel snapped and quickly leaned over the desk and reached out for the file, but not before the MP had read the name and address on the heading. 'You haven't seen the last of me, Mr Weltham.'

The MP's eyes blazed like Catherine wheels on 5 November. He leapt to his feet.

'You've had your chance, Angel,' he bellowed. 'Get out and don't come back until you've got evidence, hard, rock-solid evidence.'

ELEVEN

'Right. Let's have a look at them then, lad. Put them down there,' Angel said pointing at the desk in front of him.

Ahmed carefully placed six postcard size black-and-white photographs one at a time on the desk.

Angel eagerly peered at the slightly fuzzy pictures showing the man in the pink suit taken from the CCTV tape.

'The contrast is not very good, sir,' Ahmed said. 'There wasn't enough light.'

Angel looked closely at them, moving systematically from one print to the next.

'Hmm. I can see that. Oh dear. Hmmm.' Angel was clearly disappointed. 'For stills, I suppose they're good, but, I mean, from these pictures, I can't say with absolute conviction that this is Jones. The figure looks right. The size and shape. The suede shoes. The suit. The bow tie. But the hat and the sunglasses cover most of his face. Now, he has a distinctive mouth. Is that *his* mouth? Mmm.'

There was a knock at the door.

'Come in.'

It was DS Crisp. 'I've brought that photo back, sir.' He put a big envelope on the desk.

'Ah, it's you. At last. I thought you'd gone off on a world cruise.'

'Nay sir,' he protested.

'Have you spoken to those women?'

'Yes sir. All four of them. And all four of them say this is the photograph of Frank P Jones.'

Angel pulled a face. 'Well I know that, lad, don't I? His agent sent it to me, didn't he. Of course it's Jones. I want to know if it's the man who shot Charles Tabor!'

'Yes. They're one and the same!'

Angel shook his head wearily. 'That's what I am trying to find out!' he bellowed. '*Are they?*'

'Each one of the witnesses was seen separately and each one says that that is the photograph of the man who shot Charles Tabor.'

'Definitely?'

'Absolutely.'

'Right. Did you find out anything about the safe being robbed?'

'They didn't see anything, sir. None of them. On the afternoon of the murder, after you had interviewed them they left the factory together at the same time, about four o'clock and then made their separate ways. Two went straight home, one went shopping and the other one called on her mother and then went home. Do you want me to check on their alibis, sir?'

'Ay. Better get on with it. I am still fishing in the dark about that missing money. Get me something to work on. Anything!'

Crisp rushed off.

Angel picked up the envelope and pulled out the photograph of Jones taken in the Louvre. He compared it with the CCTV prints. He shook his head.

'Ahmed.'

'Yes sir,'

'Look at these and tell me if they are of the same person.'

Ahmed pored over the pictures carefully, then he pulled back and shrugged.

'They look the same to me, sir.'

Angel nodded, but he wasn't pleased. 'Yes. Right lad.'

'Do you want me to look the Dooley incident up next, sir?'

'Ay. Right. Push off then.'

Ahmed went out and closed the door.

Angel took another look at the photographs, selected two from the CCTV print-outs and the one in colour and marched out of his office down to the superintendent's office. He knocked on the door and heard the bark: 'Come in.'

Superintendent Harker swivelled round his chair to face the door.

'I've been looking for you,' he said sternly.

'Oh,' Angel said, trying to look innocent. 'I was out early doors, John. I've been in since ten.'

'And I've been with the chief until two minutes ago. Or else I would have come looking for you. Your time's up. In fact it was up on Friday. What are you messing about at?'

'Yes sir. I know. Is the chief pleased that all the brouhaha has moved away to the hospital?'

'Delighted,' said Harker curtly. 'Now, what *are* you messing about at? Why haven't you pushed that Jones case up to the CPS?'

'I still haven't got Mac's report on Jones's clothes, house and car. I am expecting it any time.'

'I'll sort Mac out,' replied Harker ominously. 'What's he playing about at? But that's an excuse. I gave you a direct order to get shut of this case.'

Angel thought quickly. 'Can I answer that question with a question, sir?'

'No,' snapped Harker. 'But I'll listen. Nobody can ever say I don't listen.'

'Will you have a look at these photographs?'

The super pulled a pained face and shook his head.

Angel placed the two photographs from the CCTV and the coloured one on the desk.

The super glanced at them briefly, then looked up.

'What am I looking at?' he asked.

'The question is, are they the same person?'

Harker looked again at them closely for a few seconds.

'Yes. No,' he said. Then he added tersely: 'They seem to be.'

'Yes sir. They seem to be, but *are* they?'

The super's jaw stiffened. He gripped the arms of the chair.

'Look here Mike, I don't care *what* he looks like. I don't care if he looks like Ann Widdecombe. If he shot Charles Tabor, bang him up! If he didn't, chuck him out! It's of no interest to me what he looks like. God knows, I've seen all sorts! If they're brought in here in the best suits, spats and a monocle, I don't care. If they come in, half-starved, in fashion torn jeans, with rings in their ears, pins in their noses and heroin needles up their arses, it doesn't make any difference to me, either. This isn't *Pop Idol*. If they've committed an offence, bang 'em up, and if they haven't, chuck 'em out!'

Angel was suprised at the outburst. He knew he was potentially in trouble because he had gone well past the ultimatum, but he didn't expect the superintendent to be so explosive.

'This isn't the time for nancying around with diddy photographs and wet-nursing a cardboard cut-out of a man, courted because he knows a bit about art, appears on television and wears a technicolour suit. I don't know what you are messing about at. Are you going to hand the case up to the CPS or do you want me to boot you out and do it myself?'

'I'll do it, sir,' said Angel resignedly.

'*Today!*' boomed Harker.

'Today.'

Angel didn't say another word. He collected the photographs off the desk, came out of the super's office and quietly closed the door. He was subdued and ruffled, but as he trundled up the corridor, he thought, all in all, that he had come out of the contretemps rather well. Harker could have formally reprimanded him on the spot, which would have appeared on his record. He wouldn't have liked that. There was no alternative. He would now have to wrap up the Jones case. He couldn't see the urgency. He still needed Dr Mac's report, and another day or two wouldn't have mattered much, especially as the news-gathering fraternity had totally deserted the station in favour of the hospital. This should have soothed the chief constable's nerves.

Round the corner, he met Ahmed carrying what looked like an old occurrences book.

'I was looking for you, sir.'

'What, lad?'

'That Dooley incident, sir.'

'Come in the office.'

Angel slumped into his chair at the desk, rubbing his chin. Ahmed closed the door.

'I've got the occurrences book which includes December 2003, sir.'

'That'll have to wait, lad.' Angel sighed. 'You'd better bring all the stuff you have on Jones, the videos, the exhibits, everything. And get me the CPS on the line,' he said glumly.

Ahmed's face brightened briefly, then he looked confused.

'You've solved the case, sir?'

'No lad. I haven't,' Angel replied gruffly. 'Come on. Chop-chop. Get on with it. We'll look into the Ingrid Dooley business later.'

'Right, sir.'

171

Suddenly the door opened with a flourish. It was a red-faced Superintendent Harker in his hat and buttoning up his overcoat.

'Ah, Mike,' he said excitedly, his bright eyes sparking like a welder's arc. 'I've just had a tip-off from Scotland Yard. The Home Office has sent them a signal. A drugs baron intent on operating up here in a big way has just moved into the town. I'm taking a squad up there. I want every available man and women uniformed and plainclothes on this. Now!'

Angel leapt up. 'Yes, sir. What's the address, sir?'

The super read from a piece of paper in his hand.

'It's Flat 6, 452 Sheffield Road. I'll see you there.'

He dashed off. Angel watched him run out of his office and up the corridor. Then he turned to Ahmed.

'Nip smartly into the CID room, the loo and the briefing room and tell anybody there to turn out pronto to that address,' he ordered. 'Then join me in the carpark. You come with me in my car,' he added, grabbing his coat. 'Now this'll be an entertainment!' He gave a grin.

When Angel arrived on the scene, there were four marked police cars and two unmarked on the forecourt of the new flats. As the inspector and Cadet Ahaz made for the main doors, two other police cars pulled up behind them. They entered the lift and pressed the button for Flats 5 to 8, which were on the first floor. Entry had already been effected into Flat 6, and there were a dozen policemen and two police-women swarming inside. The flats were modern, fully furnished but tiny, comprising a main room with a bed, a kitchen and a bathroom. Under the doorbell push was a piece of card with the name 'A Berk' handwritten in ink. There was little space for them in the crowded room so Ahmed stood with Angel in the corridor looking into the flat through the open door.

Superintendent Harker was in the centre of the main room surrounded by police.

'Quiet everybody,' he called. 'Quiet. Disappointing that there's no villain here, but we can wait. Now, where's the fingerprint man.'

'Here, sir.'

'Just dust these drawers.'

The police constable waved his magic brush with aluminium powder on the front of the chest of drawers and the knobs.

'There's nothing there, sir.'

Harker turned to DS Crisp and pointed to the drawers.

'Have a look in there, Sergeant,' he said.

Crisp opened the top drawer and pulled out some under-wear and some photographs. The group reacted with murmurs of delight tinged with concern when a white plastic bag of powder was found at the back of the drawer.

'Careful lad.'

Crisp carefully put the plastic bag on top of the chest. The super nodded to the constable with the brush to try for dabs. He did the business and eventually reported: 'Nothing sir.'

The superintendent then pierced the bag at the corner with his ball-point, put a moist finger on the hole, collected a few crystals and applied them to his lips.

'Mmmm. Yes. I think it's heroin.' He nodded to Crisp and pointed to the other drawers. 'See what else there is, lad.'

The sergeant pulled open the drawers and closed them in turn. They were empty.

Just then, Angel heard a commotion behind him and a voice he recognized.

'Excuse me, gentlemen will you let me through? I'm Eric Weltham, your member of parliament. Thank you. Thank you. Thank you very much.'

The MP bustled across in front of Angel and made his way into the room.

'Who's in charge here?'

'I am, sir. Superintendent Harker. What can I do for you?'

'Ah. My name's Eric Weltham. Your MP.'

'Ah yes, sir,' Harker said, recognizing him and trying to be seen as accommodating.

'I live opposite and I saw this crowd of police cars arrive; naturally I was curious to see what was happening. Now, what's going on?'

'We think we have made a drugs bust, sir.'

'Oh? Well, I want to offer my help and support if it is needed. I am always interested in supporting the police and aiding in any community matters, you know.' He saw the bag of white powder, which had been placed on the top of the chest of drawers. 'Is that it?' he asked tentatively.

'Yes,' Harker replied. 'Well thank you, sir. Thank you very much. But everything is in hand.'

'Hmm. Have you searched the place? Have you found any documents? Papers? Records?'

'No sir.'

'Oh.' Weltham looked disappointed. 'Well, who lives here, then? Who's the tenant? Who rents the place?' he puffed.

Angel pushed into the room from the doorway, followed by Ahmed.

'I do,' the inspector said quietly.

There were murmurs of surprise.

Angel strode casually across to the chest of drawers, and picked up the contents of the drawer piece by piece.

'Yes. These are my pants, my vest and my socks. These are my handkerchiefs with my initials on, look MA. My wife bought me them last Christmas. And look, this is a photograph of my wife, and there's one of my dog, Bonnie. I took these on holiday in Scarborough in July. And that's a photograph of my front garden at home. That's the new birdbath we got from Focus. Looks nice there, doesn't it?'

He turned to Eric Weltham and pointed to the alarm-clock on the bedside table. 'You see that clock? That's from the side of my bed at home. It's a good timekeeper. It's spot on. Look, three o'clock.' He turned to Ahmed. 'Tell them, lad. Tell them what you did early this morning.'

Ahmed coughed into his clenched fist.

'I came with DI Angel early this morning and brought those clothes and photographs, and alarm clock,' he said in a small voice. 'I checked that the clock was the correct time. It was. It was a quarter past eight. I don't know where the bag of heroin came from, but we didn't bring it.'

Weltham brought himself up to his full height.

'Well,' he said loudly, 'I do, and I'm not surprised. We've got a crooked policeman in our midst,' he boomed, eyeing Angel pointedly. 'A druggie who is a dealer and a police inspector at that! Superintendent, arrest that man.'

Harker looked stunned.

Angel smiled and slowly turned to Ahmed.

'Just a minute, sir. Cadet Ahaz has not quite finished, have you lad.'

'No sir.'

'Go on, Cadet. Spit it out!' Harker said impatiently.

'We also brought a vibration-operated video-camera, and set it on top of the wardrobe,' Ahmed said quietly.

Angel pointed up to the top of the wardrobe. All heads turned to look at it.

'Ay. It's there. It'll be recording this now.'

A tiny, black, shiny eye could just be seen peeping over the top of the wardrobe.

'It was deliberately placed in range to record pictures of

anyone who came into the room and also the clock, so that we would know the time. It will have recorded the person putting that bag of heroin there and the time.'

Weltham was dumbfounded. His eyes shone and his forehead glistened with perspiration.

'Your name wasn't on the doorbell,' he said, his shaking hand reaching up to his bottom lip.

'No sir,' Angel said.

'Well, who is A. Berk, then?' he asked weakly.

'I'll give you one guess, Mr Weltham,' Angel said with a smile, and slowly turned to Crisp. 'Search him. Charge him. And lock him up.'

Eric Weltham was charged with being in possession of a Class A drug for the purposes of selling for profit. DS Crisp brought him back to the station, and amidst his protests, he was processed and put into a cell.

Meanwhile, Angel had phoned through to the CPS to get the case against Frank P Jones in motion. The clerk had said he would arrange the collection of the paperwork and exhibits the following morning. Thereafter, Angel had busied himself fixing the prints from the CCTV and the large colour photograph on to his office wall with Blue-Tack. He had spaced them at eye-level facing his desk and was reflecting on his handiwork when there was a knock at the door.

'Come in.'

It was Ahmed. He had four box-files with several plastic bags on top of them in his arms.

'Where do you want these, sir?'

'On the desk, lad. On the desk. Is everything there?'

'Yes sir,' Ahmed said as he placed them all down carefully.

Angel returned to studying the photographs on the wall.

'You'd better push off. It's gone five o'clock.'

'Yes sir. Good night, sir.' Ahmed turned to go, then he stopped. 'Are you all right, sir?' he asked.

'Ay. I'm all right.' Angel sighed. 'Tired maybe. Fed up, maybe.'

'It was a good wheeze to get that politician, Mr Weltham, charged and arrested, wasn't it.'

'It wasn't a wheeze, lad. He was actually caught in possession.'

'Yes, sir.' Ahmed's smile changed to a frown. 'Now that's what I don't understand?'

Angel sighed. 'Go home, Ahmed. Go home. Your curry will be getting cold.'

Ahmed smiled. 'Yes, sir. Goodnight.'

'Goodnight,' Angel murmured, rubbing his chin and peering at a photograph.

The door closed, but was opened again almost immediately.

'What you doing?'

Angel recognized the gruff voice of Superintendent Harker. He turned round.

'Oh. Just having another look, John. That's all.'

'Ay,' Harker replied abstractedly. 'There's been a right old shemozzle up there today on the Mawdsley estate. Right outside that post office. Did you warn off all the lumps I told you to?'

Angel rubbed a hand over his mouth.

'Well I think so, John. I have had rather a lot on my plate lately.'

Harker's face went red. His eyes gleamed.

'We've *all* got a lot on our plates,' he barked. 'Tomorrow I want you to sort it out. It's top priority. There's that lump McCallister putting the fear of God into all the old folk up there. The chief has had that councillor woman, Elizabeth Mead, bending his ear most of the afternoon.'

'She's not old.'

'No. But her mother is!' he yelled. 'And she lives up there.'

'Yes. All right, sir. I'll do what I can.'

'Mike,' said Harker slowly, staring into his eyes. 'I want you to do better than you can. Oh yes. I want McCallister on a spike, wrapped up in barbed wire and transported as far away from Bromersley as possible. Have you got that?'

Angel sighed. 'Yes sir.'

The Superintendent made for the door. Then suddenly he stopped, turned back and with a smile that would have terrified Dracula, said:

'Oh yes. I just wanted to say you pulled a good 'un today.'

Angel's eyebrows lifted. 'Ah yes,' he replied. 'Well, I was never going to get him for bribery and corruption, was I.'

'Hmmm. No. No,' Harker said thoughtfully. 'I didn't know he was into heroin, though.'

'He wasn't, John.'

'Eh?' Harker, screwing up his face.

'Al Capone wasn't an accountant, was he,' Angel replied with a wry smile.

'Another day, another dollar,' Angel muttered to himself as he turned the key in the bungalow door. He withdrew it, thoughtfully, walked up the path to the garage, unlocked it and lifted up the door. Then he walked into the car, put the key in the lock. He had carried out this routine a thousand times, maybe a million, but this morning, it was different. He had used three different keys in less than twenty seconds, and each time, as he had checked the key before pushing it into a lock, something like a flash of light, had zipped across his mind. He couldn't put a finger on it. The last time he'd had this experience was the other morning, when he was shaving and a picture of Ingrid Dooley in tears in the waiting area at the police station two years ago had flashed by. Memory plays tricks on you. He didn't know what this heralded or where it was to lead.

He reversed the car out of the garage, still thinking about it, and it remained at the forefront of his mind when he arrived at the police station and pulled round the side into the carpark. He tapped the code on the panel on the back door and let himself in. When he reached his office and saw the four box-files with several polythene bags on top, stacked ready for the CPS, he rummaged through the bags to find one labelled, Exhibit 12, which was the key. The key that mysteriously opened nothing!

The phone rang.

'Angel?'

'Good morning. This the CPS. Can I send someone to pick up the paperwork for the case against Jones?'

'Oh? Ah. Yes. Tell him to ask for Cadet Ahaz, will you?'

'Will do.'

The man rang off. Angel tapped in a number. The phone was answered.

'Cadet Ahaz.'

'Is DS Crisp there?'

'No sir.'

'Right. Well, bring yourself in here, lad? We'll deal with that Dooley business.'

'Yes sir.'

Angel sat at his desk looking at and fingering the key and key-ring. He turned it every which way until Ahmed arrived with a thick journal and a bunch of papers.

'Now then. What were you able to find out?'

'Well, I've got the occurrences book, and I've made some notes from it and from a taxi driver's statement, sir. My writing's not so good. Can I read it out to you.'

THE MAN IN THE PINK SUIT

'Ay. Go on then, lad.'

'Well, from the occurrences book, sir, it said that in the early hours of the morning of the twenty-fifth December 2003, Christmas day, a man called Alec Dooley, a widower, of thirty, Park Street, died in the street outside Pewski's, the undertakers, at sixty-one Sheffield Road. A taxi driver, Barry Turner, reported it through his radio and the taxi depot manager reported it by a triple nine. Turner, the taxi driver, said he had picked up two men from the Feathers Hotel and taken the first man to the railway station, and was told to take the other chap to Pewski's. When he got there his passenger, Mr Dooley, was dead. The doctor said he had died of heart failure accelerated by an excessive intake of alcohol and the verdict of 'natural causes' was subsequently brought in by the coroner. The dead man's daughter was called Ingrid Dooley of the same address. She said that he had been celebrating his win of two million pounds on the lottery at the Feathers. However, the supposed winning ticket was never found.'

Ahmed looked up.

Angel sniffed. 'Is that it?'

'Yes sir.'

'Well, mmm. I remember seeing Ingrid Dooley that Christmas day. I must have been on duty. She must have come into the police station following her father's death, to make a statement. There was a bit of a party going on in the CID office, and although we were working, there was a seasonal atmosphere about the station. So it was a bit poignant that she was mourning the loss of her father. It mustn't have been very nice for her.'

'No sir. Did you have to deal with the dead man, sir?'

'Thankfully no. It wasn't my case. Andrew Pogl dealt with it, I think. He's retired now. Taken a pub in Anglesey. Who was the other passenger in the taxi?'

'I wondered about that. It didn't say that anywhere.'

Angel frowned. 'I wonder who it was? Mmm. I think I know how I can find out. I must go to the Feathers.'

There was a knock at the door.

'Come in.'

'You've been looking for me, sir?' Crisp asked.

'Yes. Where've you been? Did you have to have your leg amputated, then?'

Crisp's mouth opened in astonishment.

Angel shook his head. 'Never mind lad. You've been that long, I thought you must have had to go to the hospital to have your leg off.'

'No sir. I've been down the cells trying to settle Eric Weltham down. He wants his solicitor.'

'Well close the door. There's a right old draught. He can have his solicitor.'

Crisp closed the door and approached the desk.

'I'll tell him. He says it's a case of entrapment.' He smiled.

'He'll have a job on making that stick.' Angel turned to Ahmed. 'By the way, you'd better phone the hospital. Have a word with DS Gawber and see how Jones is. Do it in the CID room.'

'Right, sir,' Ahmed dashed off.

'Sit down, Sergeant. Now, how did you get on with the alibis?'

'Oh yes. They look all right to me, sir. Everything checks out. All four left the factory around four and their movements have been accounted for until well after five o'clock.'

'So there's no question of the four colluding and ganging up and cooking up some fairy-tale about what happened and what they saw?'

'None whatsoever, sir.'

'Hmm. And they were never in a position to get at that safe, either separately or in a group?'

'No sir.'

Angel nodded. He reached forward and picked up the key and key-ring lying on the desk. He looked at them again, then put them down and pushed them across the desk.

'Here. Take this. I've got a little job for you.'

TWELVE

'This is Inspector Michael Angel, Bromersley police,' he said into the phone. 'I'm in need of your assistance.'

'Anything I can do, Michael. My name is Andrew Baccarat. I am an inspector here at Dashford.'

'Yes. I think we can be mutually helpful, Andrew. They put me through to you. You've been chasing a regular customer on your manor called Alan Gledhill Taylor, aka Alan Fields and aka Jonno Fields, aged forty-four, is that right?'

'Oh yes, I have. I most certainly have.'

'What can you tell me about him? I know he's served time. He was an associate of three men who robbed an RAOC depot in north Yorkshire in 1985 and got ten years.'

'Yes. He's been in here a few times, but we never seem to get anything to stick. He's rough and dangerous. We had something on him for dealing in Class A, but the only witness we had failed to appear. Of course, he'd been got at. We've not seen the little man since. I dread to think what happened to him. Taylor comes over your way, these days, I believe. Started a loan scam.'

'That's what I'd heard. Do you know his haunts, his associates, who he lives with, his address?'

'He's a bit of a loner. He drifts hither and thither, doesn't have a regular address. Flits from girlfriend to girlfriend.

Doesn't seem to have any regular associates or dependants either. It's difficult to pin anything on him. There's nobody to let him down. He's a wily customer. He frequents the Sportsman at Hillesley.'

'Hmm,' Angel muttered thoughtfully. 'Will you e-mail me a photo of him, Andrew?'

'Certainly will.'

'Ta. Well, I've got a punter here. Harold Percival McCallister, aka Tiny McCallister, he's got a loan scam operating in Bromersley. I've got to get shut of him. He's driving my chief nuts.'

'I know the feeling, Michael.'

Angel said, 'I thought we could help each other there, Andrew.'

For the third time, Angel banged on the door of the terraced house. Then it was suddenly yanked open and a small, smartly dressed old woman appeared. She had a shock of white hair and a white craggy face with more lines than Clapham Junction. She squinted at Angel with eyes like raisins and waved her arms in the air.

'What a bloody racket!' she yelled. 'What's happened? If you're a tallyman, I don't want anything. Buzz off!'

Angel thought by the look of her face and shape of her head, that maybe there was something in Darwin's theory.

'Are you Mrs McCallister? I'm looking for Mr McCallister.'

'He's dead. Died in 1979. What are you wanting with him anyway?' Suddenly her mouth opened wide to show her stubby brown teeth. 'Are you from the insurance?'

'No. I'm looking to speak with Harold Percival McCallister. Would that be your son?'

'You're not wanting money on the chuckie, are you? That's

my department. I lend it out. I decide who has it and how much.'

A huge face appeared from behind the door. It was Tiny McCallister in a blue open-necked shirt and jeans. He saw Angel and pulled a face like a sluice man.

'He's a copper, mother,' he said. 'I'll deal with him.'

The old woman immediately turned, shoved the gorilla out of her way and scuttled into the house. McCallister dug his thumbs in the top of his jeans and strutted on to the step.

'What do you want, Angel?'

'Well, well, well, Tiny. You don't look any worse for the thrashing you had, do you.'

McCallister breathed in and stuck out his chest.

'Takes a lot to get me down. Now what do you want?'

'I've had a complaint.'

The big man rocked his head slightly from side to side.

'You always get complaints.'

'About your treatment of some of the old ladies on this estate.'

'Don't have much to do with old ladies.' McCallister smirked. 'I like them younger.'

Angel's fists tightened. He was angry but he spoke quietly.

'I've come to warn you.'

'You what?' McCallister sniggered.

'Leave them alone. It's a rotten scam you've got, lending money to poverty-stricken old folk at exhorbitant rates.'

'It's not a scam. It's a perfectly legitimate business. If we didn't lend it to them, they'd go without. Nobody else will lend them anything. Nobody!'

'They'd be better off struggling through. Once they're in your clutches they can never get paid off.'

'Oh please,' he replied mockingly. 'You'll have me crying, Inspector Big-head.'

'Well, I'm going to close you down,' Angel continued quietly.

'What I'm doing is perfectly legal.'

'It may be legal, but it's dishonest, it's immoral and it's cruel. If you won't close down this scam voluntarily, I am going to find a way to shut you down.'

'I've every right to carry on my perfectly legal business. As long as I stay within the law, you can't touch me. So go ahead Mr know-it-all Angel. Do your worst!'

'Oh I will. Rest assured, I will.'

Angel drove to the Sportsman at Hillesley that night straight from the office. It was ten miles north out of Bromersley on the A61. It wasn't much of a pub for sportsmen; it wasn't much of a place for anybody except those who wanted beer cheap and little else. He climbed uncomfortably on to a stool at the bar and ordered a glass of beer. He took a sip and put the glass down. It tasted as if it had come straight from the spillage tray from the previous night's session.

The barman was a lumpy fellow in his fifties, who was trying to look busy, wiping things, moving things, repinning cards of nuts and pork-scratchings, squashing crisp-packets, rattling bottles in crates and splashing water. All the time, his eyes were darting about looking everywhere and particularly at Angel.

There were only two other customers in the pub. They looked like workers having a drink on their way home. They sat at a small table behind him.

Angel looked at his watch: it was 7 p.m.

Several customers came in, had a drink and went out. The round black-and-white brewery clock on the wall moved slowly to 7.30 p.m.

The barman leaned over Angel's glass.

'Do you want another?'

Angel pushed the near full glass towards him.

'I'll have a whisky.' He took out a note and held it while the drink arrived.

Suddenly, the door opened behind the inspector and a big man with a tanned skin and a light-blue track-suit came in. Angel clocked his target in the mirror but didn't turn round.

The barman smiled slightly.

'Usual, Alan?'

'Ay. A pint.'

Taylor took up a position at the opposite end of the bar to Angel.

The inspector heard some muttering followed by the ring of the till.

The door opened again and DC Crisp came in. Angel saw him and quickly took something out of his pocket. It sparkled in the pub's lights. He dropped it over the bar at the barman's feet. The man looked down, then up at Angel, who shook his head slightly. Alan Taylor also saw what had happened. He quietly stuck his nose into the glass of lager.

DS Crisp strutted up to the bar. The barman tried for a smile.

'What can I get you?'

The sergeant stared through him.

'I just want a word with this gentleman.' He turned to Angel, jerked his head towards the door. 'Won't keep you a minute, sir.'

Angel licked his lips, said nothing, climbed off the stool and walked slowly to the door.

They went out to the small carpark at the front.

Taylor found a piece of window he could look through to watch what was happening. Outside, Angel started shouting at Crisp who then shouted back. Next thing Angel emptied his

THE MAN IN THE PINK SUIT

pockets on to the car bonnet, Crisp fingered quickly through it. There were more angry exchanges. Crisp had the last word and Angel stuffed his possessions back into his pockets. Crisp pointed a masterful finger at him, and then pointed at the pub.

Angel started for the door followed by Crisp.

Taylor had returned to his place at the bar.

Angel came in looking cool, climbed silently back on to the bar stool.

Crisp looked round the room. There were only three customers besides Angel and Taylor. Crisp approached the barman.

'Has this person been trying to sell you anything?'

'Nope,' the barman said, drying a glass off with a tea-towel. Crisp looked at the others.

'Has this person been trying to sell you anything?'

'No,' they all replied, including Taylor.

The sergeant looked slowly round the little bar at the staring, blank faces, then giving a long look at Angel, he suddenly snapped, 'Right,' and strode straight out through the door.

Angel listened until Crisp's car was out of earshot, then he sighed, picked up his glass, drained off the whisky and nodded to the barman to refill it.

'Here. You dropped this,' the barman said with a grin and handed him a heavy-looking gold chain about forty-eight inches long.

'Ta,' Angel said smiling, and stuffed it quickly into his pocket.

The other drinkers and Taylor gathered round him.

'What you got?'

'Gold chain,' Angel said.

'Let's have a look.'

Angel pulled it out and draped it on the bar.

'What carat is it?' said one of the men.

'I bet it's eighteen,' said another.

They all had their fingers on it and began to feel it and gently pull at it.

'What's it weigh?'

'Don't know.'

'Is it pinchbeck?'

'No. It's gold.'

'What do you want for it?'

Angel pursed his lips. 'Six hundred quid,' he said boldly.

'Let me see,' Taylor said reaching out for it.

'Ay.'

'Lot of money.'

'Too much.'

'Is it hallmarked?'

'Don't know. I expect so.'

'It's hallmarked there, look.'

'Oh ay.'

'It's very worn.'

'It's old. How old is it?'

'It's antique.'

'It's worn.'

In a loud stentorian voice, Taylor suddenly said:

'I'll give you a hundred quid.'

Angel shook his head. 'No.'

At that, the men began to drift back to the tables. Angel picked up the chain from the bar and stuffed it back in his pocket.

Taylor was rubbing his chin slowly.

'I could go maybe to a hundred and fifty.'

'No,' Angel said abruptly.

Taylor brought his glass and sat on the stool next to him.

'Where'd you get it from?'

'Mmm. Roundabout,' Angel answered vaguely.

'You're not a dip?'

'Certainly not.'

'It's nicked though, isn't it?'

Angel hesitated, and then said, 'No.'

'You've served time, haven't you?' Taylor winked and nodded encouragingly.

'Might have,' Angel said, trying to look nonchalant.

'You *have*. I've seen you.'

'I don't think so,' Angel said indignantly.

'I have. It was in Durham.'

'No.' Angel knew he must be careful. Taylor could have been laying a trap. He knew he'd served time in Armley.

'Doncaster?'

'No.'

'Wakefield?'

'No.'

'Armley?'

Angel smiled.

'Ah,' Taylor said triumphantly. 'I knew you were an old-timer. Hmmm. What landing were you on?'

'Second.'

'I was on the second. What were you in for.'

'You ask a lot of questions.' Angel emptied his glass. 'I must be going.'

'No. Have another.' Taylor turned to the barman. 'Give him another, Jeff.'

The barman whipped his glass across to the optic.

'I really should be going.'

Taylor rubbed his chin again. 'I bet you're a con artist.'

Angel smiled.

Taylor continued: 'You're dressed the part. Smart suit. Collar and tie. Polished shoes. Smart haircut.'

Angel smiled again.

Jeff placed the whisky and water in front of him.

'Well thank you,' Angel said. 'But really I shouldn't. I'm driving.'

'Where do you live?'

'Bromersley.'

Taylor's face changed. 'Bromersley?' He thought about it for a while. 'I'd got you down for Headingley.'

'No,' Angel said. 'Let me ask a question.'

'What?'

'Where do *you* live?' Angel picked up the glass.

'Chapeltown.'

'Coincidence. I know a man in Bromersley who knows a few chaps from Chapeltown.'

'Big place,' Taylor said, taking a gulp of lager. 'What's his name?'

'Big man. Funny that. He was saying how he knocked ten bells out of a man who fancied himself as a bit of an athlete. Had a big head. Trying to muscle in on his loan business, he said. On the Mawdsley estate in Bromersley.'

Taylor's mouth dropped open. His eyes wavered uncertainly from side to side and then settled.

Angel noticed this with satisfaction.

'There's a lot of cream there, you know,' he continued. 'Lots of biddies with pensions. Gave him hell. I would have liked to have seen him running, crying all the way down that canal. Middle of January, it would be. *He* came from Chapeltown. You might know him. P'raps not. As you say, it's a big place.'

Taylor's face was scarlet, his jaw set like a steel trap, his icy blue eyes narrowed and his vision blurred with rage. He tried to speak, but couldn't.

'Is there anything wrong?' Angel asked.

'What's his name?' Taylor managed to ask eventually. 'Dammit! What's his bloody name?' He screamed and banged his fist on the bar.

'Er … Tiny McCallister, as a matter of fact.'

'McCallister!' bellowed Taylor. 'I knew it!'

The men on the tables behind looked up. The barman looked worried.

Angel tried to look concerned. 'That's the chap. He lives on—'

'I know where he lives!' Taylor ranted. 'I know where he lives!' he railed. 'But not for much longer, he don't!'

Angel pushed into the interview room, looked round, wrinkled his nose and threw a file of papers on to the table.

'Phew! What a stink!' he said to Ahmed and quickly crossed to open a window. 'Have there been some flowers in here, lad? You don't want flowers in an interview room. This isn't the BBC. We're not interviewing Catherine Zeta Jones.'

'It's nothing to do with me, sir.'

A lady in a blue overall carrying a bucket and mop passed the door. Angel saw her and leaned out.

'Excuse me, love. Have you been putting flowers in here?'

'No I haven't,' she said resentfully, in a voice like Robin Cook having a flu jab. 'Not since one of your big nobs complained.' She put the bucket down. 'You try to make things nice, and what do you get?'

'Oh, you do make them nice, very nice,' Angel said quickly. 'Everything shines like a new penny. But there's always a smell in here.'

'There's no pleasing you lot,' screeched the cleaner. 'Well I won't bother trying to make it nice in there then. In fact, I won't even bother going in. I'll cross that room that off my list! You can scrub it out and polish it.'

She picked up the bucket and started down the corridor. ' I don't have to take all this,' she muttered, as she trundled along. 'It wasn't like this at the Co-op. I cleaned there for eight years and never a complaint. What's the matter with them? You do your best and try and make it nice and see what happens.'

Angel stood in the doorway, scratching his head. Ahmed watched the woman shuffle along, her voice echoing down the corridor.

'Men are queer enough, but police are worse. I've never liked this job. I should have taken that job at the library. I wouldn't have to put up with all this. It's disgraceful. If my mother was alive, she'd turn in her grave.'

They watched her disappear round the corner, then looked at each other. Angel went back into the room and sniffed the air.

'Mmmm. That's better. Right lad. Show Miss Dooley down.'

'Yes sir,' he said and ran up the corridor.

Angel sniffed approvingly round the room, switched on the tape-machine, muttered something into it and opened the file. The long-legged lady in thigh-boots and with jet-black hair appeared at the door. Angel stood up.

'Miss Dooley. Please come in.' He indicated the chair.

'Thank you,' she said with a smile that showed off her dimple. 'It's Inspector Angel, isn't it.'

'That's right,' he said affably, and then he deftly mimed to Ahmed to close the door and take a place at the table. 'We are recording this, Miss Dooley. It's just a formality. Thank you for coming in to see me.'

'It's a pleasure, Inspector,' she said as she took a chair and lowered a Harrod's shopping bag on the floor by her side. 'Now what did you want to see me about?'

'I want to ask you about the murder of Charles Tabor on Monday the seventeenth of January. It was at approximately eleven a.m. Where were you at that time?'

'I don't know exactly. I know I was on an errand to the dispatch office, to do with …' She broke off. 'You have already asked me about this, you know, Inspector.'

'I know. I know. But if you wouldn't mind going through it again.'

'Well, I had to organize the dispatch of a part in the post that day as the customer had been promised.'

Angel ran his tongue across his lips. 'And where were you when the actual shot was fired, then?'

'I didn't hear it. I must have been on my way back to the office.'

'So you were downstairs?'

'Yes. I must have been, because when I got back it had only just happened. Mr Tabor had been shot. The girls were in hysterics. I asked one of them what had happened. She told me. I dialled 999. Then I phoned Mark's office on the factory floor. He wasn't there, so I told the girl to find him and ask him to come up urgently. That's about it.'

'And when did Mark Tabor arrive?'

'Oh, he came up a minute or two later, and then after what seemed an endless time, the ambulance men arrived and then you were close on their heels.'

'Then what did you do?'

'I met you. You asked me what I had seen, and you wanted to use my office. Don't you remember? I went for a walk.'

'It was so cold.'

'It was.'

'What time did you get back?'

'About five o'clock.'

'Was the office empty?'

'No. Mark Tabor was there.'

'Where were the safe keys?'

'On the desk, I suppose. I can't say I noticed.'

'So you walked about the estate in all that weather for more than an hour?'

'I suppose so.'

'You didn't go anywhere else?'

'No.'

'The other members of the general office had gone home.'

'Yes. Apparently.'

'Leaving Mr Tabor's office unoccupied.'

'Mark Tabor was there.'

'All the time?'

'Yes.'

'How do you know?'

'Well, I don't.'

'He was at the hospital, with his father.'

'Oh yes.'

'All the staff left early on that day.'

'I believe so.'

'And what time did you leave?'

'I left with Mark Tabor.'

'And what time would that be?'

'About half past five.'

'Mark Tabor had to lock up that night. There was nobody else?'

'No.'

'What did you do while he was checking the doors and the lights?'

'I didn't do anything.'

'You just sat in your office and did nothing?'

'Well, yes.'

'I'll tell you what I think you did,' Angel said coolly. 'You took the keys off the desk, opened the safe, took out all the money in there then locked it up again. In the region of a hundred and five thousand pounds and put it somewhere safe, probably your desk and some in that bag you have down there, which you took home that night. The following day, you took home the rest.'

'No,' she said firmly, her big eyes staring at him.

'Yes,' he said with a nod.

'You can't prove it.'

'No. Not yet. You hated Frank P Jones, didn't you?'

'No.'

'It was his fault your father lost his ability to play the violin. Wasn't it?'

'Who told you that?'

'Mrs Tassell.'

'Oh!'

'She told me that he pushed your father over.'

'He broke his wrist. It stopped him earning a living,' she said angrily. 'It shortened his life! If it hadn't been for Frank P Jones he would have still been here!'

'Thereafter, you had to support him. Financially, I mean.'

'I had to support him in every way. He lived with me. He was depressed. He used to drink. I was the only breadwinner.'

'Things were difficult?'

'Very.'

'But your father had some savings?'

'No.'

'A pension?'

'No. Unemployment pay, that's all.'

'And your earnings at the factory.'

'Yes.'

Angel rolled his tongue round his mouth. 'How did you manage to buy that brand new car? Must have set you back thirty thousand pounds. That solitaire ring. There's five thousand. Those boots three hundred.'

'I had *my* savings.'

He smiled wryly. 'What you saved out of your salary from Charles Tabor?'

'Yes.'

Angel sighed, then slowly shook his head. 'It won't do, Ingrid. It won't do. It doesn't add up right.'

He noticed her chest heaving. She licked her lips and stared right back at him. Angel pressed on.

'Charles Tabor must have been paying you remarkably well.'

'Enough.'

'Perhaps you had a relationship that was more than employer and employee?'

She gave the slightest shudder. 'No. Certainly not,' she replied. Her eyes flashed wildly. 'No.'

Angel knew that was the truth for certain, or she was an excellent actress. He thought he would try another tack.

'You're a very handsome woman, Miss Dooley.'

She didn't react. He went on: 'How tall are you?'

She hesitated. 'Five feet, eight inches.'

'Do you know how tall that man in pink is?'

She looked mystified. 'I have no idea.'

'He's five feet, eight inches.'

She shrugged.

Angel nodded. 'What a coincidence.'

THIRTEEN

Angel was looking closely at the photographs stuck on the wall of his office. He flitted from one to the other and back to the larger coloured photograph of Jones in the Louvre, holding the famous drawing by Leonardo da Vinci. He was looking for that telltale sign, that inconsistency, that piece of information that was going to indicate whether the photographs were all of the same man or not.

There was a knock at the door.

'Come in,' he muttered.

It was Ahmed. 'Oh. You're back, sir.'

'What do you want, lad?'

'You asked me to phone the hospital and find out how Mr Jones was.'

'Ay. And how is he?'

'DS Gawber said he was off the drip, been out of bed, had some breakfast. He's been chatting to him. He could be coming home in a few days.'

'Oh? That sounds a lot better. Is Gawber all right?'

'Yes, sir.'

'Hmmm. I must go down there.'

Ahmed grinned. 'Huh. You'll need an escort, sir. Did you see the photograph in the *Daily Standard*, all that crowd round the hospital doors?'

'Oh. It's like that still, is it.'

The phone rang. He reached over the desk. 'Angel.'

It was the superintendent. 'I've got Mac's report. You'd better come.'

'Right, John,' Angel replied enthusiastically. He slammed down the phone, and made for the door. Then he turned back, pointed at the wall, looked at Ahmed, and said, 'I'm going to see the super. Take a shufti at these pictures. See if *you* can find a difference. The prize is a bottle of Glenfiddich.'

Ahmed's mouth opened, and his eyes followed him down the corridor.

'I don't drink, sir,' he called after him.

'Oh no. A case of Pepsi then.'

Angel knocked on the superintendent's door.

'Come in, Mike,' Harker called. 'Sit down.'

'Yes sir.'

'I've read it.' Harker picked up a bunch of six A4 pages, heavy with print and stapled at the corner. He handed them to him and then rubbed his chin with a big red hand.

Angel took the report and stuck his nose into it.

Harker sniffed and after a moment said, 'I'll tell you what it says.'

'Hmmm. What?' Angel mumbled, turning over a page.

'It says there were no powder marks on the suit. No blood specks. Nothing foreign on the shoes. No positive footprints anywhere in the factory or the offices. No related fibres. Nothing.' He wiped his hand across his mouth. 'In short,' he said, 'Jones didn't shoot Charles Tabor.'

'Hmm.' Angel looked up. He smiled. 'I'll tell him.'

The corners of Harker's mouth turned down as if his piles were playing up.

'You better inform the CPS at once. And the press will have

to be told we've dropped the charge. You'll have to issue a statement.'

Angel lowered the report. The two men looked across at each other briefly.

Harker glowered. 'Where do we go from here?'

Ahmed was still perusing the photographs as Angel came back into the office. 'You'd better pack that in, lad. We've a lot to do,' he said as he pulled out the swivel-chair and looked down at the desk.

Ahmed turned to the inspector.

'You can't see his right hand in this photograph, sir,' he said.

'What,' said Angel, abstractedly; his mind was on other things. He pulled open a drawer.

'He's holding a drawing or something.'

'Yes. By Leonardo da Vinci. So what?'

'You can't see if he's wearing a ring.'

Angel thought for a second. 'Well, he is. I've seen him wearing a ring. A plain wedding-band.'

'Yes sir. It's on the stills taken from the CCTV. The ones I did.'

'Yes? So what?'

'Well, is he wearing a ring now?'

'Yes, he is. I've seen it. It was too tight. He couldn't get it off.'

'Well I can't see it, sir.'

''Course you can't. You've just said. He's holding that picture.'

'Ah! But is it on the same finger?'

'What?' Angel stopped fishing in the drawer and looked ahead at nothing in particular. He was thinking out what Ahmed had said. The lad was right to question it. Jones was certainly wearing a ring on his right hand, on his second or third finger. But he couldn't say for certain which one.

'Hmmm. Well, it doesn't matter now, lad. Forensics say he didn't do it. I'm dropping the charges.'

Ahmed looked surprised.

'I thought you knew that, sir,' he said. 'That's why you didn't want to bring the CPS in, and were looking so closely at Ingrid Dooley.'

Angel sighed, then nodded. 'All right. Ring DS Gawber at the hospital, and ask him to check on that wedding-ring. Find out which finger Jones is wearing it on.'

Ahmed made for the door.

'Ay,' Angel called after him. 'And get him to take it off,' he added artfully. 'Tell him I want it as evidence!'

'Right, sir.' The door closed.

Angel picked up the phone. 'Get me the CPS, please.'

He explained to the CPS about the late and conclusive forensic evidence and it was arranged for their messenger to return all the papers and exhibits the following day. He then began drafting a statement to circulate to the press and media. This wasn't as easy as it would seem. Although he had to tell the absolute truth, he also had to try to put the Bromersley police force in the best possible light, and head off embarrassing and intrusive questions. Consequent upon his arrest for this dramatic and unusual theatrical murder, Jones was now so newsworthy that this announcement would inevitably command an enormous amount of attention locally, nationally and abroad. Angel knew he needed to be very precise. The statement was taking some sort of shape, when Ahmed knocked on the door and noisily dashed into the office.

'Sir! Sir!'

'What is it, lad? What ever is it?'

'I phoned the hospital. Mr Jones is wearing that ring on the *third* finger of his right hand. The *third* finger, sir!!'

Angel beamed. 'Good. Good.'

'And he can't get it off, sir. He can't get it off,' said Ahmed excitedly. 'Even the nurse can't get it off! She's rubbed his finger all over with petroleum jelly. Do you want them to saw it off?'

Angel pursed his lips. 'No,' he said rubbing his chin. 'No. If ever he's got to count up to ten, he'll need it.'

The following morning, at 8 30 a.m., Angel left his bungalow and went straight to Bromersley General Hospital. It was a cold morning and there had been a slight frost but there was still no snow. He reached the hospital in good time despite the morning rush hour, and parked beside a white television van with an aerial dish on its roof. As he went through the revolving door, he noticed that there was still a substantial press pack in hibernation waiting for news of the man in the pink suit. Men in heavily creased raincoats, youths in jeans and trainers, monopolized the sixteen seats, and another ten or twelve held up the wall in the reception area, and had cameras and recording machines at their feet. They were mostly reading newspapers and making the tea-dispensing machines and the telephones work overtime.

Angel made his way surreptitiously to the lift and pressed the button for the fourth floor. When it reached the level and the doors slid back, he spotted Constable Scrivens along the corridor sitting on a chair next to a door. When the young man saw the inspector, he recognized him, stood up and began to button up his jacket.

'Everything all right, lad?'

'Yes sir.'

'Everything quiet?'

'It is now,' Scrivens said meaningfully.

'Where's DS Gawber?'

'Inside, sir. With Mr Jones,' he said pointing to the door behind him.

Angel nodded.

'Are you going in, sir?' the young man asked.

Angel nodded. 'Ay. That's what I'm here for.'

Scrivens opened the door and Angel walked into the little ward.

Frank P Jones was sitting up in bed. He shuffled himself up the bed expectantly and straightened the sheet. The appearance of Angel seemed to energize him.

'It's you,' he said. 'At long last you have deigned to visit me. I thought you would have been here before now. I was sure you hadn't finished with your wretched questions.'

'No sir, not quite,' Angel said affably. 'It's a policeman's stock in trade, you know.'

Beyond the bed, DS Gawber was lounging on an easy-chair. He saw Angel and, employing an elbow crutch, began to struggle to stand up. Angel waved him down. 'Now then, and how are you, Ron?'

'Getting better, every day, sir.'

'Good.'

Angel surveyed the room. It was white and spotless. One wall was all windows, on another wall was a sink. There was a bedside cabinet loaded with bundles of envelopes and packets bound in rubber bands, a pile of newspapers and a jug of water and a glass. Protruding from under the bed was a cardboard box also filled with bundles of unopened envelopes and packets. There was a black metal-and-plastic chair against the wall.

Jones's face was a lot paler than when Angel had last seen him in the interview room at the station, but he was looking perky. He was sitting up in the bed, wearing pink pyjamas, and had half-lens spectacles perched on the end of his nose. There was a newspaper with a huge photograph of him across the front page laid on the bed.

Angel reached out for the chair, dragged it to the side of the bed and sat down.

Jones looked at Angel with doleful eyes.

'More questions, Inspector?'

'I have some very good news for you, Mr Jones.'

'Oh? What's that?'

'We are dropping the charges.'

Jones's mouth opened. He didn't look pleased; he rubbed his chin. He looked suprised.

'Oh.' His eyes moved unsteadily from side to side then came to rest looking into Angel's. 'That means, I am free to go?' he asked tentatively.

'As far as the police are concerned there is no case to answer. We will not be pressing any charges,' said Angel with a smile. 'When you are fit, you can leave hospital and do what you like. I am withdrawing police supervision immediately.'

DS Gawber, who had been listening, smiled.

'Does that mean I can step down, sir? I'd like to go home.'

'Whenever you like, Ron. And thank you for stepping in. Get that ankle rested.'

'I will.'

Jones turned to him. 'And I thought we were getting along so well.'

Gawber nodded. 'Yes sir. We were.' He struggled to his feet and put the crutches under his arms

'Leave discreetly Ron,' said Angel. 'Don't let that press pack realize you're going. When this news breaks, I expect there will be all hell let loose. Tell Scrivens what's happened but tell him to keep his trap shut. Tell him to hang on for ten minutes after you, and then leave quietly for the station.'

'Right.' Gawber reached the door. 'Goodbye, Mr Jones. I hope you go on all right.'

'Thank you, Sergeant, and thank you for your company.'

'Goodbye Ron. See you soon.'

'Goodbye, sir.' He opened the door. The constable assisted him out of the room and closed the door.

'That police sergeant has been a delightful companion,' remarked Jones. 'He knows nothing about Picasso, though.'

Angel smiled. 'There are a few questions, Mr Jones.'

Jones nodded. 'I have one for you, Inspector,' he said. 'I told you from the very beginning that I knew nothing about the shooting. What finally convinced you?'

'Primarily forensic evidence. Your pink suit was not the suit worn by the man or woman who shot Charles Tabor.'

'I told you that.'

Angel nodded. 'You told me all sorts of things,' he chided. 'You told me things that were not quite correct. For instance, you told me that your garage was locked at the time and it wasn't. And you wouldn't tell me that the key that was found was for the garage door. I mean, why say that? What was the point?'

'Ah,' Jones responded, pointing a finger skyward. 'There's a good reason for that, Inspector. The newspapers are printing everything you know, every detail. If my insurance company had discovered that I had told them the car was normally locked up in a garage when it wasn't, it might have invalidated the insurance. I lost the key a month or so back. I had intended sorting it out but I've been so busy. Besides that, Inspector, you were being extraordinarily annoying with your questions.'

Angel shook his head. 'It's a little thing like that that could have put you behind bars.'

Jones smiled. He put his hands together on his lap, touching and separating at the fingertips in quick succession.

'And another thing,' said Angel. 'I asked you where you got the diazepam tablets from, that were in your pocket. You said you hadn't seen a doctor in years, then you said they were prescribed for you, then you said you bought them in Holland. But you didn't, did you?'

'Oh dear,' Jones replied, looking worried. 'I really cannot afford to get mixed up with anything illegal you know, Inspector. Especially drugs. Oh dear no. That would never do. And everything, every little detail is reported in the papers. If the papers learned I had drugs, look what a big thing they would have made out of it. It could have ruined me. No. The truth is, I was protecting a friend. Well, he's not exactly a friend. I meet him from time to time in a studio I occasionally work in. He recommended them, and said he could get some for me. I don't want to get him into trouble. He was helping me, you see. I really do not want to give you his name.'

'You should have said so. I will not pursue the matter, in this instance, provided that you promise me to see your GP about the matter and get a legitimate prescription from him.'

'Oh, I will. I will. And thank you.'

The door opened and a young nurse put her head round. She saw Angel but ignored him.

'Are you all right, Frank?' the nurse said in a voice that had the resonance of a cracked cup.

His eyes lit up. 'Oh yes, thank you, nurse,' he said extravagantly.

'Do you wanna cup of tea?'

'No, thank you.'

'Is there anything you do want?'

'No, thank you.'

'That man's rung up from California, again!' she said with a big grin.

Jones shrugged. 'Never mind!'

The door closed. Jones smiled at Angel.

'Interruptions like that, all day,' he chuckled. 'When I get out of here, I'm going to have to get a full-time secretary.'

'Looks like she's got a year's work ahead of her, answering all these letters,' Angel said, pointing at the box under the bed and the pile on the bedside locker.

'You know, Inspector, I never expected that morning eleven days ago, when you came to my house and accused me of murdering Charles Tabor, that as a result of that mistake – an understandable mistake – my life would be transformed like this.'

Angel shook his head. 'You are out of the woods. But I still have to find the murderer of Charles Tabor. And there is one very serious question I have to put to you. This is probably the last question I will ever have to ask you.'

'Hmm. What is that, Inspector?'

Angel scratched his head. 'Somebody wants you put away. Out of commission. Silenced. In prison. Yes. Who is it, Mr Jones? Who is your enemy?'

Angel left the hospital at 10.15 a.m. He drove straight to the Feathers Hotel and went up to the reception desk. A big woman aged about thirty came forward.

'Can I help you, sir?'

Angel put on his best Roger Moore smile.

'I'm sure you can. I am Inspector Angel of the Bromersley police. I would like to see the receptionist who was on duty on Christmas Eve two years ago.'

'Two years ago?' echoed the big woman. 'Oooo. That was the night of the storm, very heavy rain, wasn't it. I nearly got pneumonia. I was on duty, Inspector. I was on duty all night until six o'clock Christmas day morning. We were fully booked and very busy; well, we always are at Christmas.'

'Ah, good. There was a gentleman here, at the bar that night, celebrating a rather spectacular win on the lottery.'

'Oh yes. The poor man died. Mr Dooley. On his way home. Died of natural causes. Yes I remember, Inspector.'

'He was celebrating somewhat spectacularly. Had a lot to drink. Champagne, I expect.'

'No, it was brandy, Inspector.'

Angel was pleased. She remembered; that was good.

'Brandy, was it?'

'I told all that I knew to the police at the time, and his daughter, poor woman. Ingrid, I think her name was. Yes. He was a widower, you know. It was very sad. Him winning all that money, two million pounds and then dying the same night, never to touch a penny. Mind you, she would be all right. All that money. She came to see me, you know. I told her all about it, everything I knew. But it *was* natural causes, you know. The coroner's verdict was that. Oh yes. Natural causes, he said. Yes. I helped put the gentleman in the taxi.'

'Oh yes?'

'Yes, Inspector.'

'And who went with him in the taxi? Who paid the fare? And gave you a big tip to keep your mouth shut?' he sniffed.

Her eyes stared angrily at him, and her fat red lips tightened.

'There was no need to say that! Well, it doesn't matter now, anyway. He's dead. It was Charles Tabor.'

There was the link, the link Angel had been seeking, someone who hated both Frank P Jones *and* Charles Tabor. Hated them enough to see Charles Tabor shot dead and Frank P Jones sent to prison for life.

It was Ingrid Dooley.

Angel got in his car and drove straight up to Tabor's factory. He went past the receptionist, up the stairs along the landing to the secretary's office. The door was open and he walked straight in.

Ingrid Dooley was seated at the desk shuffling papers around. She looked up and smiled.

'Hullo Inspector.' She dropped the papers and cut the smile when she saw his face. 'You want to see me. Sit down, Inspector.'

Angel came right up to the desk, put his hands on the top of it and leaned forward.

'Why didn't you tell me that Charles Tabor stole your father's lottery ticket?'

'How did you find that out?'

'The same way you did. Did you take on this job to get your own back, to kill him?'

'No.'

'Was it to get at his son?'

'No. No! He got my father drunk, so drunk that it killed him, and while he was drunk, he stole the winning lottery ticket from him. That was two million pounds. A fantastic amount of money for the likes of my father! We had always rubbed along managing on a hand-to-mouth existence, and then came the chance to break out of the rut, to have a nice house, car, new clothes, holidays, all that I had dreamed of. No more worrying about money. And it was all taken away by this ...'

'So you took a job here to get your own back.'

'I came here to keep an eye on him. I was hoping I might get enough evidence to prove he stole it, and recover the money. I know it was a long shot, but to me, it was worth trying. That money would have revolutionized my life. But the man was evil. Do you know what else he did?'

'No.'

'There was a man in the accounts department here. He made a mistake. A trivial thing. It was soon put right. But Charles Tabor wanted rid of him. He not only sacked him, he played a dirty trick on him. He got him to sign away his rights to his notice, his holiday pay and his pension rights for five thousand pounds, which he duly paid him in cash. He then arranged to have him robbed of the whole lot on his way to pay it into his bank!'

'Can you prove it?' .

'It's true. His name was Coldwell. I was here, in this office. I heard the whole thing. And do you know who Tabor set on to rob him?'

'No.'

'A well-known local crook, McCallister, Tiny McCallister. You must have heard of him.'

Angel blinked. 'McCallister. Oh yes. I've heard of McCallister.'

'He did all his dirty work.'

'Did he? Did he? All right. Why did Tabor tell the taxi driver to take your father to 61 Sheffield Road, Pewski's the undertakers?'

'A cynical joke. A cruel and sadistic act. Typical of Charles Tabor.'

'You know, Miss Dooley, the person who shot Tabor and had Jones blamed for it, was somebody who had reason to hate them both. I can't make it all fit yet, but you are the only person in the world I know of who fills that bill. The stake was high. And it wasn't only for a hundred and five thousand pounds, it was for all this.' He waved a hand in the air.

Her mouth opened wide. 'Ridiculous! Who could I have got to dress up as Jones and kill Charles Tabor?'

Angel glared at her.

'You could have done it yourself.'

FOURTEEN

A ngel was excited when he reached the office the following morning. Even though it was Saturday, he was exhilarated having unravelled a mystery as confusing as this had been. It was during watching a television programme with his wife the evening before, about a celebrity-programme presenter bitching about another celebrity-programme presenter, that the last cog had dropped into place.

This morning, he plunged enthusiastically into assembling the facts of this latest murder, in sequence, for his report to the CPS.

He was still in this euphoric mood when the phone rang.

'Angel,' he sang into the mouthpiece

'This is Mark Tabor. I'm very worried, Inspector. Ingrid Dooley has cleared out her desk. I went through it this morning looking for something. Looks like she's done a bunk!'

Angel's face dropped. 'Oh?'

'Yes. She's disappeared. She's been so reliable. I phoned her home, but there was no reply. I am very dependent on her since Dad died. I went immediately round to her house. There's this morning's post sticking out of the letter-box and the house certainly looks unoccupied. A neighbour said he'd seen her last night put two suit-cases in her car and drive off, but I can't think where she's gone. I thought she would have told me. I can't think what's happened.'

Angel sighed. 'Oh. Thanks for letting me know, Mr Tabor. I'll have my sergeant look into it as soon as possible.'

Angel wondered if the superintendent had come in. He immediately went down to his office.

Harker was there in a track suit.

'It's predictable. With all that brass the girl can go anywhere. Put out a notice in the *Police Gazette*, circulate the airports and the national dailies.'

Angel nodded. 'With her looks and in that car, she'll not get far.'

'It's rough that she was done out of her father's lottery winnings,' the superintendent said, being uncharacteristically compassionate. 'But she can't flout the law and run away like that.'

'If she returns most of the money, pleads guilty, gets a good barrister to make an effective case in mitigation, and the judge sees she's genuinely remorseful, she'll be treated sympathetically, won't she.'

'Maybe. But not if it's Judge Keeler.'

'I could even put a word in for her, myself.'

Harker looked as if he'd just knocked the top off an addled egg.

'Don't go mad, lad. Just because she's a bit of a looker!'

The inspector had just returned to his office when the phone rang.

'Angel.'

'It's Crisp, sir.'

'What you doing here, lad? I thought you'd be off tormenting the women of Bromersley?'

'I'm duty sergeant, sir. There's that woman from the television, Louella Panter. She's asking to see Eric Weltham. She's got some post and fruit and stuff for him, and she also wants to see you.'

Angel sighed.

'Ay. All right. Bring her down to the interview room.'

He replaced the phone, went straight out of the office, and down the green corridor. He opened the interview-room door and found the room predictably stuffy and uncomfortably warm as usual. He crossed to the windows, opened them both, and switched on the recording machine. He heard footsteps along the corridor and turned to see DS Crisp, Louella Panter and Nigel Coldwell file silently into the room. He thought she looked shorter and tubbier than he remembered. She was wearing a light-coloured trouser-suit and her hair was in an organized jumble like a pineapple on the top of her head. Her lips and cheeks were very red as if she had applied her make-up in a hurry. She was carrying a shoulder-bag, holding on to it with one hand.

Following her into the room was Nigel Coldwell in a smart suit with a light-blue shirt open at the neck. He carried a big canoe-shaped basket of fruit and had a bundle of envelopes and newspapers in an elastic band tucked under his arm.

Angel felt hostility in the air, but he did his best to be affable.

'Good morning. Please sit down.'

Louella and Nigel both muttered: 'Good morning. Good morning.' The man put the fruit and papers on the table.

Angel looked across at Crisp.

'Come in, Sergeant, and close the door.' He pointed to a chair.

When the four were sitting at the table, Angel said:

'Now then, Miss Panter, what did you want to see me about?'

Louella touched both corners of her mouth with her middle finger and began in a businesslike manner.

'I want to know what's happening with Mr Weltham, Inspector. I mean, you know he has absolutely nothing to do with drugs.'

'The videotape showed otherwise, but if he can give a satisfactory explanation to the judge then he has nothing to worry about,' Angel answered, deviously. 'And by the way, this conversation is being recorded, so anything you say may be used in evidence.'

Louella's lips tightened. She ignored the caution.

'But it was a trick, Inspector. You know it was.'

'It's up to a judge and jury to decide that.'

Her eyes shone with rage.

'But you fixed it! You manoeuvred him into that position!'

Angel felt his chest rise and swell.

'What are you talking about,' he said glaring at her. 'An honest man couldn't be manoeuvred. I didn't manoeuvre him. I didn't invite him into the flat. He broke in. I didn't plant a kilo of heroin with the intention of destroying a man's career! And that's what his motive was, you know. He would have cut me down without a thought. My reputation to me, is as important as his reputation is to him. And I don't accept bribes either! I know this is a time of crisis for you, Miss Panter! I know that your relationship with Eric Weltham is on the wane.'

'It isn't,' she snapped, her eyes flashing angrily.

Angel waved his hand impatiently. 'If you don't mind me saying so, you are not the slim beauty that had first caught his eye three years ago. You have a slight weight problem, don't you. You can't keep slim. Well, regrettably, some of us carry a few pounds more around with us as we get older. We may not like it, but we put up with it. But for you, it's very different. Oh yes. Your appearance is your stock in trade. Glamour is your business. If you're not glamorous, the TV mandarins won't want you.

'And that's part of your trouble, isn't it? But only part. Your new series isn't going down too well, is it? Audiences are not flocking to switch it on like they used to. The viewing-figures are slipping. If they don't hold up, your career in television could be over. As it is, your fellow celebrities have started gunning for you. You are forever spatting with local art man Frank P Jones. There are tit-bits all over the papers. And you know that once you become a figure of fun, it snowballs and every tin-pot personality, announcer and pub comic joins in with the jibes!

'But let's go back a bit. When Eric Weltham and you first met, you were both doing rather well. He was an important man: a respected cabinet minister. You were earning a fortune on the box. You two bunked up together, and with your joint resources, began to live in style. You met important people. You both mingled with the famous from governments, both British and foreign, as well as entertainment stars and celebrities. You travelled with him, discreetly, abroad, holi-dayed together. I expect you had visions of being a cabinet minister's wife. Everything was hunky dory until you found out that your lovely Eric had accepted money from Charles Tabor for inside government information, and that now Tabor was blackmailing *him*, and getting all the money back and more!

'This drain on your resources began to affect your life style: the trips became limited, the parties were getting fewer, at the same time, your celebrity status was diminishing and work was slower coming in. If there was any more bad publicity, your television career might be over. Also your spats with Frank P Jones were coming more frequently. And you were envious of him, particularly when he got any publicity locally, and you didn't. Overnight, the sequence of glamour, success, TV work, celebrity status and money was grinding to a halt. You saw these two people, Charles Tabor and Frank P Jones as the cause, and you decided to have them removed.

'So you, or Nigel here, or both of you, had this brilliant idea: to dispose of the blackmailer by shooting him, and have your irritating rival blamed for it. Well, you only had to wiggle your hips, give one of your well-practised smiles and make a few empty promises to Nigel here, and he'd slay a dragon for you, and he'd do it in style. And that's what happened. So you cooked up this vicious scheme to dispose of two very different types of birds with one stone.

'Nigel had a motive too. His father had been unceremoniously both sacked and robbed by Charles Tabor on the same day, two years ago. I only found out about that by accident, yesterday. You already had a gun bought by Nigel a year ago from a regular customer of mine, Irish John. Jones had a similar figure, was the same height, and his face and hair would virtually be covered by the hat and the sunglasses. You thought it would be a 'hoot' and you could polish off two enemies for the price of one. You engaged Mrs Tassel innocently to make Nigel a made-to-measure cream suit and you dyed it pink. I found the dye container in your dustbin area at the back of your house. You even stuck a wedding-ring on his right hand. Pity you didn't get the correct finger. You picked a fresh carnation from the greenhouse, and after he'd got dressed up, you drove him to the factory, where he went into the building and shot Charles Tabor. He then surreptitiously returned to the car and you drove him back home.

'Later that same day, while you disposed of the clothes, Nigel went to watch Jones's house. You knew the police would be there, and when he saw me cart him off to the station, he went into his garage. Luckily, he didn't need to force the door. It wasn't locked.'

Angel turned to face Nigel who was sitting there with his mouth open.

'You opened the car with a strip of metal from a packing case like a practised car thief, and put the gun under the seat. You know, lad, even an innocent like Frank P Jones would have known to dispose of the gun in a pond or somewhere and not leave it placed so easy for us to find. Then you sneakily dropped the used carnation buttonhole in the dustbin.

'Do you know Nigel, that was your biggest mistake. If you had done your homework, you would have discovered that Frank P Jones suffers from allergies. In particular, he can't live near pollen. The slightest whiff triggers his asthma. He could never have worn a natural flower! Yes, on the telly, he always wore a carnation, but it was *artificial*.'

Angel stood up. He could feel his pulse thumping, he knew his face was red.

Louella Panter and Nigel Coldwell sat in stunned silence. Angel turned to Crisp.

'Search 'em. Charge 'em. And lock 'em up.'

That night, Angel slept the sleep of the just; it was the best night he'd had for a fortnight. The next morning was Sunday, a day of rest. He took his wife to see her mother in Bridlington, had a walk round the harbour, sunk three halves of Old Peculiar in a bar overlooking the sea, had a fish-and-chip tea in York and was home in time to see *Last of the Summer Wine* at 6.15.

On Monday morning, he couldn't wait to get to the office. He wanted to finish writing his report and pass up to the CPS the case of the man in the pink suit, as it became famously known. He reached the office by 8.20 and sifted through his post. There was a small white packet, addressed personally to him. He opened it carefully with a penknife he kept for such jobs. Inside was a small piece of cake topped with pink and white icing, and a handwritten ivory card. It read:

To Inspector Angel. Please accept this piece of cake to celebrate the marriage of (Irish) John Holmes to Kathleen Docherty at the Feathers Hotel, Bromersley. Saturday, 22nd January. We done it by speshul liscence.

Angel smiled and shook his head. He closed the box and carefully put it in the drawer.

There was a knock at the door.

'Come in.'

It was Ahmed, with his eyes bright, wearing a big smile. He was eagerly waving a piece of paper.

'What's that, lad?'

'It's an e-mail, sir. It's about Ingrid Dooley.'

'Oh yes. Well, come on, lad, what's it say?'

'It's from the Met. A patrol spotted her car in Knightsbridge, in London, yesterday. They stopped her, arrested her and she's being held at Paddington Green. They want someone to go down and collect her.'

'Hmm. Good. I'll send Crisp. When you see him, tell him I want him.'

'Yes sir,' Ahmed said and left.

The phone rang. He picked up the handset.

'Angel.'

'This is Inspector Baccarat from the Dashford force.' He sounded happy.

'Ah,' Angel said, his eyes opening wide with expectation. 'What's the news, my friend? Did it work?'

'Like a dream. Your customer, Tiny McCallister, is in hospital in Leeds General with a broken arm and collarbone, and we've charged Alan Taylor with GBH and causing an affray. With a bit of luck he'll get five years.'

Angel smiled. 'Good. Good. That'll keep McCallister out of the chief's hair for a bit too. I'll tell him.'

'I thought you'd like to know. We followed him to the house, as you said, and waited until he came out. He was only in there about five minutes. Then we arrested him and sent for an ambulance for McCallister. I want to thank you.'

'It's a pleasure. Any time. Goodbye.'

There was a knock at the door.

'Come in,'

It was Ahmed struggling in with a big cardboard box. By the look on his face, it was heavy. Angel looked up.

'What have you got there, lad? Put it down before you do yourself an injury.'

Ahmed put it on the chair by the door. 'Don't know, sir,' he puffed. 'Just come. Got a label on it. It's addressed to you. Delivered by van.'

Angel stared down at the box.

'Mmm. Oh, yes. No lad, it's not for me. It's for you.'

Ahmed's eyes lit up. 'For me, sir?'

'It's nobbut my dues and demands, Ahmed. It's a case of Pepsi. I never go back on a deal.'

'Oh. Thanks very much, sir.'

'Aye. Well, leave it there for now and hop it. I've a lot on this morning.'

'Yes sir.' Ahmed went out and closed the door.

Angel made substantial progress in reducing the pile of papers on his desk. He completed his report on the murder of Charles Tabor and assembled all the documents, statements, tapes and exhibits for Ahmed to take to the CPS. At length, he took off his reading glasses, rubbed his eyes and looked up at the clock. It was 12 noon: lunch-time and he was ready for it.

He decided that, for a change, he'd go to the Feathers. He fancied a big piece of game-pie and a half of Old Peculiar, and the walk through town would be a welcome change after being cooped up in the office all morning. He put on his coat and gloves and made his way up the corridor, through the reception area to the front door.

It was a cold, January day, but the sun was shining and had burned away the early frost. He had gone out of the station door and started briskly down the steps when he saw a large pink car turn the corner. It was a chauffeur-driven Rolls Royce which had been sprayed pink. It was quite a spectacle and the few pedestrians on the quiet street stopped and stared at the phenomenon as it made its stately progress towards the police station. Angel watched the limousine glide to the kerb and stop ten yards ahead of him. He continued to stare as he went down the steps. By the time he'd reached the pavement, the passenger window had moved smoothly downward and Frank P Jones's happy face was smiling at him from the car.

'Inspector Angel,' he called, removing his straw-hat and adjusting the pink bow tie.

Angel's jaw dropped, then his face changed into a smile.

'Hello, Mr Jones. This is a big surprise. You're looking very – er – fit? When did you get out of hospital?'

'Fit as I'll ever be. I was discharged yesterday. I must keep away from every kind of flora and, I'm told, I will be absolutely fine. I'm going away for a little break, so I'm glad I caught you. I have come to thank you, Inspector, for getting me off the hook. You have said some pretty outrageous things to me, during my stay in your jail, but I realize it was all for my own good. And I appreciate your acts of fair play, and consideration throughout. I must have been a great pain.'

A woman with two small children passed by and stared open-mouthed at the pink limousine and its unusual passenger peeking through the window. Jones smiled at them and doffed his hat. The woman smiled; the children turned away. A car passed by, the driver tooted his horn and waved; Jones waved back.

'However, my detention in your primitive accommodation was not a total waste,' Jones went on. 'There have been several positive improvements in my life and my outlook over the last ten days or so has changed spectacularly. You could say, in fact, my life has been revolutionized. I now see everything in a new light! I don't think I shall ever take anything seriously again. For that, I thank you.'

Angel smiled and shook his head.

'You're welcome.'

Jones held out his hand. Angel shook it and squeezed it.

'Thank you. Thank you again, Inspector. Well, I must go. I shall be late. I have to catch a plane to the United States. Meeting a man, called Hiram something or other. Drive on, Tompkins. Goodbye Inspector Angel. Goodbye.'